Horace McCoy was b   1897. At the age of twe   ⌐y, and later served eightee   the U.S. Air Service, where he was   ..ng his lifetime he travelled all over the S   ..s salesman and taxi-driver, and his varied career also included reporting and sports editing, acting as bodyguard to a politician and bouncer in a dance contest, doubling for a wrestler, and finally writing for films and magazines. A founder of the celebrated Dallas Little Theatre, his other novels include *They Shoot Horses, Don't They?* (1935), *I Should Have Stayed Home* (1938), and *Kiss Tomorrow Goodbye* (1948). He died in 1955.

Also by Horace McCoy
and published by Serpent's Tail

They Shoot Horses, Don't They?
I Should Have Stayed Home
Kiss Tomorrow Goodbye

No Pockets
in a Shroud

Horace McCoy

**MIDNIGHT
CLASSICS**

Library of Congress Catalog Card Number: 97-81172

A complete catalogue record for this book can be obtained from the
British Library on request

First published in the USA and Great Britain in 1937

This edition first published in 1998 by Serpent's Tail,
4 Blackstock Mews, London N4

Website: www.serpentstail.com

Typeset in 10pt Times New Roman by Avon Dataset Ltd
Printed in Great Britain by Mackays of Chatham

10 9 8 7 6 5 4 3 2 1

For Helen

1

WHEN Dolan got the call to go up to the managing editor's office he knew this was going to be the blow-off, and all the way upstairs he kept thinking what a shame it was that none of the newspapers had any guts any more. He wished he'd been living back in the days of Dana and Greeley, when a newspaper was a newspaper and called a sonofabitch a sonofabitch, and let the devil take the hindmost. It must have been swell to have been a reporter on one of those old papers. Not like now, when the country was full of little Hearsts and little MacFaddens beating drums and printing flags all over their papers and saying Mussolini was another Caesar (only with planes and poison gas), and that Hitler was another Frederick the Great (only with tanks and homosexual pyromaniacs); and selling patriotism at cut-rate prices and not giving a good goddam about anything but circulation. (Gentlemen, we are very sorry we cannot lend you our trucks this afternoon to move the loot from the City Hall, but we simply must deliver our night final. After six o'clock we will be very happy to let you have them. Or: oh yes, sir, Mister Delancey, we understand perfectly. Those two women *wandered* in front of your son's car. Oh yes, sir, hahahahaha! That alcoholic odour on his person was from somebody *spilling* a cocktail on his suit.)

'The yellow bastards,' Dolan said to himself, meaning the newspapers, going into Thomas's office, the managing editor.

'Where'd this story come from?' Thomas asked, holding up two sheets of typewritten copy paper.

'That story's all right,' Dolan said. 'That's one story that'll stand up.'

'I didn't ask you that. I asked you where you got it.'

'I got it the day before yesterday. At the last game of the series. Why?'

'It sounds pretty fantastic – '

'It not only sounds pretty fantastic, it is pretty fantastic. When a pennant-winning ball club deliberately throws a championship series for the benefit of a few gamblers, that's what you call pretty fantastic. I suppose you're going to throw that story away too?'

'I am – but that's not the only reason I sent for you. Forget the story. The business office – '

'Wait a minute,' Dolan said. 'You can't forget a thing like this. Hell, the ball club's crooked. Everybody who saw the series knows they were in the can. They weren't even clever about it. Besides, that story's not exclusive with us. The other papers have got it too – they're using it this afternoon. We've got to protect ourselves.'

'Oh, I don't think they'll use it,' Thomas said. 'Maybe this is not as terrible as you think it is.'

'It's as terrible as the old Black Sox scandal. Baseball would be in a swell fix today if nobody had printed that story, wouldn't it?'

'And Landis still would be just another judge. Now look, Mike,' Thomas said soberly, 'there's no sense in us having these arguments every time you want to vent your personal spleen on somebody. You know the policy of this paper – '

'Sure, sure, sure. I know the policy of this paper. I know the policy of every paper in town. I know the policy of every goddam paper in the country. There's not one inch of gut in all of them put together.'

'Why are you always going out of your way to offend people? Why are you always trying to kick up a stink?'

'I'm not trying to kick up anything. That story you threw away is NEWS! You're always throwing away news. Last week it was the Delancey kid – '

'We played that story down, because there is no sense in ruining a fine kid's life – '

'Well, good God, *he* ruined a couple of fine lives. He got drunk and went clear across the street into the safety zone to kill those women. Yes, sir, he had to work like hell to bag that pair. Of course, we played the story down. The fact that his old man is one of our biggest advertising contracts had nothing to do with it – '

'You're too quixotic,' Thomas said.

'Is that what it is?' Dolan said, pressing his thin lips together. 'What was it a couple of weeks ago when I brought in that story about the reorganization of the Ku Klux Klan?'

'The Ku Klux Klan is dead. That was not the Klan.'

'All right, all right, the Crusaders then – or whatever the hell they call themselves. A rose is not the only thing you can call by another name and get the same odour. They wear sheets and helmets and hold secret meetings – '

'I've tried to tell you before that no newspaper in town can touch that Crusader angle. That is pure dynamite. And the sooner you give up these reformer ideas the better off you'll be too.'

'For God's sake, don't keep telling me I'm a reformer,' Dolan said angrily. 'People can do anything they like right out in the middle of the street for all I care. That's unimportant. But what *is* important is printing some news about these political high-binders and about the big-time thieves ... why, even the goddam Governor of this state is crooked, and you know it. What happened to that story I brought you last year that a drunken Congressman had given me – with his sworn affidavit? You threw it away. All right, the hell with that now. But you've got a story in your hand about a ball club selling out, and I give you an argument about printing it and you remember all those other arguments we've had about stories, and you think I'm a reformer. How about those hundreds of kids who go out to the park every day and make heroes of these same crooked ball players – literally worship the ground they walk on? How about them?'

'That's quixoticism,' Thomas said. 'Sit down and cool off.'

'Hell. I won't ever get cooled off. This is no newspaper, this is a goddam house organ.'

'All right,' Thomas said grimly. 'I've let you pop off like this, because I thought you'd make up my mind for me if I gave you a chance. Up to now I've had some hope for you. I've put up with your belligerency and your profanity, because I thought sooner or later you'd get wise to yourself. I've been fighting just as hard as you have – to keep the business office from firing you. A dozen times they've asked me to let you go. You don't think so, eh? Well, take a look at this,' he said, reaching over into his communications box. 'Read it – '

THE DAILY TIMES-GAZETTE

INTER-DEPARTMENT COMMUNICATION

To Mr Thomas	*Date*	10–3
From Mr Womack	*Subject*	Michael Dolan

Mr Luddy of Display called on O'Hearn Sporting Goods yesterday about their new contract. This is, as you know, one of our best accounts. O'Hearn flatly refused to talk new contract, because Dolan has been owing his firm $154.50 for more than a year for golf balls, tennis rackets, golf clubs, etc. He feels, and rightly, that if he is going to do business with this paper, our employees ought to pay what they legitimately owe him. I wish you'd see me about this.

'I'm always getting notes from the business office about bills you owe our advertisers,' Thomas said.

'Slightly ironic,' Dolan said, laying the note back in the box. 'The business manager wants me to pay my debts – apparently it never occurred to him that this paper owes some debts too. Some debts to the public – '

'I'm not going all over that again,' Thomas said, a note of finality in his voice. 'I guess maybe we just can't see things the same way. Maybe I'd be doing you a favour if I fired you – '

'You can't fire me,' Dolan said. 'I don't work here any more – '

He was cleaning out his desk when the door opened and Eddie Bishop came in. Bishop was the police reporter, fifteen years on the beat. He looked like Pat O'Brien would look if O'Brien were really a reporter. He had a girl with him.

'What's this, what's this?' Bishop said. 'I hear you've quit.'

'I did,' Dolan said, looking at the girl standing beside him (the office was so small that three people filled it pretty full), thinking how red her lips were, the reddest lips he had ever seen on anybody.

'Meet Myra Barnovsky,' Bishop said. 'You ought to know Mike,' he said, winking slyly.

'I've seen you in some Little Theatre plays,' Myra said, extending her hand. 'You weren't bad.'

'Thanks,' Dolan said politely. When he touched her hand he shivered and his shoulders twitched. He was embarrassed, but the girl apparently paid no attention . . .

'What was the fight about?' Bishop asked.

'Oh – same old thing. Another story he wouldn't print.'

'Well, I envy you having the nerve to quit,' Bishop said. 'I envy the hell out of you. Weren't for the wife and kids I'd have told Thomas years ago where to stick this gutless gazette of his – '

'Don't let us interrupt you,' Myra said to Dolan. 'Go ahead.'

'I'm practically finished,' Dolan said. 'I was just cleaning out some junk – '

'What are you going to do now?' Bishop asked.

'I don't know. First of all I've got to make up my mind whether I'm glad this happened or whether I'm sorry.'

'Look out, now,' Myra said, aiming her finger at him straight from those red, red lips; 'don't weaken – '

'You're glad,' Bishop said. 'Take it from me, you're glad. At least you've got your self-respect back.'

'What's left of it,' Dolan said, looking at him, trying to smile. He liked Bishop. He had always liked him. Bishop was his friend. Bishop was the sort of friend you could go to and ask how to pronounce hard names like Goethe and Beethoven without him laughing behind your back. He wished now, suddenly, that Bishop had come in alone, without Myra Barnovsky (he wondered who she was and where she had come from and why she made him feel so funny), so he could have sat down with him and confessed that his smile and his indifference were faked and that he really felt panicky and helpless inside, and that because this was the only job he knew, maybe he'd better go back to Thomas and apologize and promise to be a good boy in the future and keep his mouth shut. But Bishop hadn't come in alone, he had brought Myra Barnovsky... 'Yes,' he said, 'what's left of it – '

'You'll be okay. We'll see you for lunch,' Bishop said, starting out.

'I don't think we'd better leave him,' Myra said. 'He's on the verge of going back to his boss and apologizing and begging for his job back. Just to be sure he doesn't, we'd better take him with us – '

Dolan turned around and looked at her in astonishment.

'Don't be surprised,' Myra said. 'There was nothing difficult about it. It's written all over your face. It's strange how these things work out,' she said to Bishop. 'If I had been one minute later getting out of bed this morning, if I had stayed in the johnny one minute more, if I had missed that particular street car, if I had stopped to get my usual cup of coffee – and why didn't I stop? That's odd, because I haven't missed my morning coffee in years – if I had been one second longer doing any of those things, if I *had* stopped for the coffee, I would have missed seeing you. And if I had missed being here Dolan undoubtedly would have gone and begged for his job back. And he would have gotten it, too. But now he won't. He's finished with this. Don't you think that's odd?' she asked Dolan.

'I suppose so . . .' Dolan said, shivering again, looking at her with the look of a man who knows the woman he is looking at is his for the asking, and that lying on the bed with her clothes off, her body will be beautiful and demand loving, and he knew, too, or he sensed (which are one and the same thing in sensual philosophy) that the act itself would be no more satisfactory than taking a beautiful corpse for a mistress.

It was this that startled him, and now he knew why he had shivered when he had touched her hand, and all of a sudden he was aware of what this girl had been trying to say in that confusing speech about how she had happened to be here. She had been confused, too, and had said it badly, but now in this split second he understood. She had felt the same something he had felt. Suppose she *had* stopped to get that cup of coffee . . .

'I'm ready,' he said, picking up his stuff, starting out.

Myra Barnovsky stopped him at the door. 'Take a good look around,' she said. 'You won't be coming back here any more . . .'

The three of them had lunch at the Rathskeller, and later that afternoon Dolan went over to the Keystone Publishing Company to see George Lawrence. This was a firm that printed trade magazines for insurance and hardware and implement and motor-car companies . . .

'Here's what I wanted to see you about, Mr Lawrence,' Dolan said. 'You've got a big printing shop here, and I've got what I think is a big idea. I want to start a magazine.'

'What's the matter with the newspaper business?'

'Nothing. I quit. I wasn't getting anywhere.'

'What kind of a magazine've you got in mind?'

'Oh, one a little like the *New Yorker* – maybe not quite so sophisticated. I haven't got the whole thing set in my mind yet, but I'd play up the society angle and amusements – with an occasional topical article that told the truth.'

'The truth about what?'

'Oh, anything that happened to come along. Politics, sports. Sort of keep an eye on things and look out for the people.'

'That's more in the province of a newspaper, isn't it?'

'Theoretically, it is. But none of them do it. They're afraid. Only they call it diplomacy.'

'Not a bad name for it,' Lawrence said. 'How many copies would you want? What quality paper would you use?'

'Wait a minute,' Dolan said, 'you evidently don't understand. I don't want to pay you to put out this magazine. I want you to put it out and let me edit it and write it.'

'I certainly didn't understand,' Lawrence said, frowning. 'I don't want the responsibility of publishing a magazine. It's too much of a headache.'

'You wouldn't have any responsibility,' Dolan said. 'I'd take all of that.'

'I'd be paying for it, wouldn't I? What do you call that?'

'You'd furnish the paper and print it, but I'd take care of all the rest. Distribution and advertising and the copy – '

'I'm sorry, Dolan. I don't think I'd be interested.'

'But, Mr Lawrence, you're the only man in town who's got the equipment to do a job like this. It wouldn't cost you much – you've got the paper and the machines – and a magazine like this will make a hell of a lot of money. Of course, there's such a thing as the four hundred thousand people in this town getting Justice, too – but I'm not going to talk about that, because you're a business man, and this is a business proposition. If you back this magazine for me, I'll guarantee you two thousand circulation on the first issue. That's a lot of circulation, isn't it?'

'It's considerable,' Lawrence admitted.

'And it'll go a hell of a lot more than that,' Dolan said. 'I'll rip this town wide open. You can't tell me people won't read it.'

'Sounds as if you might be biting off more than you can chew,' Lawrence said.

'Well, somebody has to bite it off,' Dolan said grimly.

'You'd make a lot of powerful enemies – '

'Sure, you would. Look here, Mr Lawrence, do you realize that a magazine like this would probably be preserved for posterity in the Smithsonian Institute? Why, there's not a single goddam newspaper or periodical in the whole country that's playing fair with its readers! They're all subsidized by advertising contracts or political affiliations – why, for God's sake, this is the greatest opportunity you'll ever have in your life! Sure, we'll make enemies. We'll make enemies out of all the crooks and thieves. But the decent element will be for us.'

'The decent element is not in power,' Lawrence said.

'Well, by God, we'll put 'em in! Don't get the idea,' Dolan said, hurrying on, a little alarmed by the frightened look in Lawrence's face, 'that I intend to devote the whole magazine to raising hell. In the main, it will be a social magazine appealing to the Weston Park crowd. But every once in a while we'll roll up our sleeves and really get to the bottom of things.'

'Dolan, I'm in perfect sympathy with your ambitions. But I can't afford it. I simply haven't got the money to take a chance.'

'How much do you think the first issue would cost?'

'Why, I haven't any idea.'

'Well, roughly, how much?'

'How big would you want it?'

'The size of the *New Yorker*. About twenty-four pages.'

'Let me see,' Lawrence said, frowning, mentally calculating. 'Around fifteen hundred dollars for two thousand copies.'

'Well, suppose I got fifteen hundred dollars together and paid for the first edition and it went over. Would that prove anything?'

'It might – '

'If the first edition was a success, would you be interested?'

'I might – '

'See you later then,' Dolan said, going out.

That night, between scenes of the rehearsal of *Meteor*, he cornered Johnny London in the dressing-room. Johnny London was but two generations removed from the log-cabin settlement that had grown into the great metropolis that was now Colton – and the twenty-storey London building now stood on the exact spot of his grandfather's hut.

'Now, what the hell is fifteen hundred bucks to you, Johnny?' Dolan said. 'You got all the dough in the world.'

'You're nuts,' Johnny said. 'You're absolutely nuts. I'm damn near broke.'

'I hate to ask you to help me out again, but fifteen hundred bucks is only a drop in the bucket to you – and it means everything in the world to me.'

'What are you going to do with that much money? What do you want it for?'

'I want to start a magazine. If you'll let me have it I'll sign half-interest over to you.'

'Un-unh. I can guess what that magazine'll be like. What about your newspaper job?'

'I quit,' Dolan said. 'I quit this morning.'

'The hell you did!' Johnny said. 'You shouldn't have done that, Mike. Hell, you were on your way to being famous. Everybody in town read your column – look, here's your pal, David,' he said, dropping his voice.

'Fellows, please cooperate,' David said, sweeping into the dressing-room. 'The last act is about ready to start, and you should be out there with everybody else waiting for your cues.'

'We came back here because we had a little business to talk over,' Dolan said.

'Well, now that you've quite, quite finished, will you get on stage?'

'But we haven't quite-quite finished,' Dolan said.

'We're coming,' Johnny said.

'Thank you so very much!' David said, sweeping out.

Dolan growled. 'He forgets this is a Little Theatre. He forgets we're not getting paid for this.'

'Don't let him annoy you. He can't help being that way.'

'I don't mind him being a pansy. It's his goddam arrogance that gets me.'

'He doesn't mean anything by it. As a matter of fact, he admires you. But, look, you'd better get out there. You're the big star, and you're supposed to set a good example for the rest of these amateurs.'

'What about the dough? Will you let me have it?'

'I'll talk to you after rehearsal.'

'It means a hell of a lot to me, Johnny.'

'*Dolan!*' a voice shouted.

'That's the Major,' Johnny said. 'Come on . . .'

'Could I speak to you a moment, Dolan?' the Major called from the audience.

'Sure,' Dolan said, going down over the footlights to where the director was sitting with David and a couple of other stooges.

'Do you realize we've only got six more days' rehearsal?' the Major asked.

'I know that,' Dolan said.

'There's a tremendous lot of work to be done. I wish you'd do your part.'

'I will – '

'I'm producing this play especially for you. For two seasons you've been begging to do *Meteor*, and now I think the least you can do is to be ready for the curtains and cues. That's only common politeness.'

'I was only talking to Johnny London a minute – '

'That's no excuse for rudeness.'

'I'm not deliberately trying to be rude. I've got a lot of things on my mind.'

'Well, get up there and try to keep this play on your mind.

All right,' the Major called to the people on stage. 'Last act! . . .'

The rehearsal was over a little before midnight.

'Well, it wasn't good and it wasn't bad,' the Major said. 'You can do better. Please brush up on your lines. Especially you, April. Tomorrow night, seven-thirty. Good night, everybody.'

' "Especially you, April," ' Dolan said to her, as the cast broke up and started drifting around.

'You weren't any too hot yourself,' April said. 'Of course, you were good in one scene. You still have one big scene left. You're marvellous in that.'

'I am pretty marvellous in that one,' Dolan admitted. 'I make a swell corpse. But I do wish you'd weep over my chest and not over my face during that heart-rending monologue of yours. I've told you before I don't like the taste of your tears.'

'I'll try to remember that, Michael,' April said gaily.

'You'd damn well better remember on opening night, or I'll bust your scene wide open. I mean it,' he said seriously. 'Am I taking you home tonight? I mean, am I taking you up to your drive-way and letting you out where your father can't see me?'

'You brought me, didn't you?'

'I met you at the drug-store. Anyway, I didn't know whether your blue-blooded fiancé was coming by to get you. Or did he get through with his business conference? God,' Dolan said, laughing, 'he's starting early. Nothing like breaking 'em in properly.'

'Where are we going tonight?' Johnny London asked, coming up.

'Home,' Dolan said. 'April has a headache.'

'Have I?' April asked innocently.

'Haven't you?' Dolan asked, winking behind Johnny's back. 'Yes – '

'That's too bad,' Johnny said to her. 'And on your one night off, too.'

'Do you mind waiting a minute?' Dolan asked April. 'I want to talk to Johnny.'

'All right – '

'Johnny,' Dolan said, walking into the wings with him, 'what about that dough?'

'Here comes your pal,' Johnny said.

'. . . Excuse me,' David said. 'Could I see you a minute, Mike?'

'Sure, you can see him,' Johnny said, moving away.

'Er – Mike, I understand you're looking for some money,' David said. 'I understand you need fifteen hundred dollars.'

'Hey,' Dolan said, surprised. 'What'd Johnny do – broadcast it?'

'He only told me,' David said. 'Do you still want it?'

'Yes, I want it, but – '

'Don't think about it any more then. I'll let you have it in the morning.'

'Well, thanks, David – you sort of embarrass me . . .'

'How?'

'Well – you and I aren't – well, we're not exactly pals, you know.'

'That's your fault,' David said. 'I'm not a bad guy in spite of what some people think.'

'No, I guess you're not,' Dolan said. 'You know what I want the money for?'

'Johnny told me.'

'I'll cut you in for a half-interest of my interest – '

'No, you don't have to do that.'

'But – well, I'd like to. I'd like for you to have some kind of contract or something. Of course, the magazine may go over – but there's always the chance that it won't.'

'I'll take the same chance you do,' David said. 'Drop around the theatre in the morning and I'll have a cheque for you. Or would you rather have the cash?'

'Either one,' Dolan said, still surprised. 'Look, I want this money more than I ever wanted anything in the world. But I think it's only fair you should know what kind of a reputation I've got – '

'Maybe I do know,' David said, smiling. 'You owe everybody in town money. You probably couldn't raise ten dollars from all your friends put together. You couldn't get five cents' worth of credit from any store in town. And I'll tell you something else. Johnny didn't ask me to lend you the money. He only told me you'd asked him. He thought it was a good joke that you'd think he was sucker enough to let you have it.'

'How'd you know all this about me?' Dolan asked.

'Everybody knows it. That's why you're having so much trouble with your Weston Park romances. The rich fathers of these beautiful débutantes have absolutely forbidden them to go with you. Did you know that?'

'I knew a couple of them had – '

'You're famous and notorious at the same time. You're *l'enfant terrible*. You've got a mania for getting into jams. You're in a constant state of rebellion. That's because you're ambitious, because you're trying to outgrow your environment.'

'Say, wait a minute,' Dolan said, dumbfounded.

'It's true,' David went on calmly. 'But you've managed to slide by thus far on your personality. You've got colour. You're attractive. You've got the physique of a Greek god. Answer me one thing: why did you ever start coming around the Little Theatre?'

'I don't know – '

'I'll tell you. Because it's got things to give you. Instinctively, you knew that.'

'Mike!' April called.

'Coming!' Dolan said. 'Look, David, I appreciate what you've said – '

'You appreciate it, but you won't pay any attention to it,' David said, smiling. 'Go on with April. Drop by the theatre in the morning, and I'll have that for you.'

'Thanks,' Dolan said, reaching for David's hand. 'Thanks very much . . .'

'I'm here any time after ten – '

'Thanks,' Dolan said. 'Thanks very much . . .'

'I felt like a heel taking the money,' Dolan said to April, as he drove her towards Weston Park.

'I don't see why. It's only a loan.'

'Well, I do anyway. I always disliked him. I hate to be obligated.'

'Because he's queer? Poor bastard, he can't help that.'

'That's not it either. I don't know – it was the shock of him offering it to me, I guess. He's the last person in the world I'd have thought of asking.'

'I understand he's very rich. His people come from Rhode Island. Whyn't you ask me for the money?'

'I owe you dough now.'

'And I'm probably the only one you owe who's collecting, too,' April said, laughing.

'I guess you are at that,' Dolan said, laughing, too. 'If you hadn't loaned me the money to make the instalment, the finance company would have this car now. How about a hamburger?' he asked, jerking his head to the Hot Spot, a drive-in shack, the midnight and early-morning rendezvous for the younger set.

'Suits,' April said.

'. . . Everything on it?' Dolan asked, cutting off the motor.

'Everything – unless – '

'Two hamburgers and two cokes,' Dolan said to the waitress.

'Everything on them?' the waitress asked.

'I should say not,' Dolan said, laughing. 'Cut the onions on both of them.'

'You know,' April said, when the waitress had moved away, 'sometimes I wonder why I didn't marry you.'

'God knows I tried hard enough,' Dolan said, 'but your old man had other ideas. I thought he'd have a haemorrhage the

day he called me up to his office and read the riot act to me.
Did he pick out Menefee for you?'

'That's not nice, is it?' April said. 'Roy's very attractive – '

'And he's got a good job and he comes from good stock and
he's president of the exclusive Aster Club. And a Phi Beta from
Yale. I know all that. But who picked him?'

'I met him when I was going to school in New York.'

'Er – confidentially, is he as good as I am?'

'What do you mean?'

'Nix,' Dolan said. 'You know what I mean.'

'Mike, you're an awful son of a bitch,' April said. 'Confidentially – no.'

'That's encouraging,' Dolan said. 'Well, this time two weeks
from now you'll be married. And Menefee'll be holding that
beautiful body of yours in his arms, and I'll be home calling
him all the dirty bastards I can think of.'

'Now, you're acting.'

'The hell I am. I mean it. Somehow, I wish this thing could
have worked out between us. I'm not in love with you, April –
but, God, I think you're swell. It's too bad I come from south
of the slot.'

'Oh, cut it out, Mike. That had nothing to do with it.'

'You think it didn't? I'm a bum. My old man is a clerk in a
dry-goods store. Who the hell am I to want the wealthy April
Coughlin? Say, when your old man pulled that crack on me I
damn near busted him one.'

'You're only being dramatic. I don't like you when you're
this way. There's Jess and Lita!'

'Where?'

'Right beside us – hello,' April called.

'Howdjedo, Lynn?' Lita said, kidding. 'Howdjedo, Alfred?'
she said, getting out of the car, followed by Jess. 'You know
Miss Fontanne and Mr Lunt, don't you, Mr Allen?'

'Hello!' Jess said.

'Hello, egg,' Dolan said.

'How're rehearsals?' Lita asked.

'Fine,' April said.

'You should see April cry,' Dolan said.

'Hey, Mike,' Jess called, motioning for him to get out of the car.

'Excuse me,' Dolan said, sliding out from under the wheel and going to where Jess stood at the back of the car.

'Mike,' he said soberly, in a half-whisper, 'we had that meeting tonight – '

'Tonight?' Dolan said, surprised. 'I thought it was tomorrow night.'

'No, it was tonight,' Jess said slowly.

'Well, when you shake your head like that I don't need to ask how I came out. Buck up, Jess, old boy,' Dolan said, a little sarcastic. 'Don't take it too much to heart.'

'I'm sorry, Mike – '

'It's all right. I've been blackballed before. So,' Dolan said, almost to himself, 'the distinguished Aster Club would have none of me!'

'I want you to know, Mike, that I was for you. But it only takes one black ball – '

'That's all right, Jess. I was a goddam fool to make application in the first place.'

'Jess,' Lita called, sticking her head around. 'Will you come here and order?'

'Thanks, anyway, Jess,' Dolan said.

'April tells me you've quit the paper,' Lita said to Dolan, as he slipped back under the wheel.

'Yeah.'

'Does that mean you'll give up broadcasting the wrestling matches?' Lita asked.

'I suppose so.'

'That's too bad, I used to stay home just to listen to you.'

'Pardon me,' the waitress said, brushing past Lita with the sandwiches.

*

'What the hell do you care whether you get into that lousy
Aster Club or not?' April asked, as they rolled through the great
stone archway of Weston Park, the entrance to The Promised
Land. 'Most of the fellows in it are snobs – coasting on their
fathers' importance.'

'I know that,' Dolan said. 'Just the same –'

'Forget it,' April said, taking his right hand, putting it
between her knees. 'Forget it,' she said softly, squeezing his
hand with her knees.

'All right,' Dolan said happily, pressing her leg with his
fingers, 'this is swell. I don't know what I'm going to do when
you get married.'

'You forget,' April said, baring her teeth a little, 'that I'm a
nymphomaniac . . .'

They were lying together on the banks of a small brook on an
old tartan Dolan always carried in his car. They had their clothes
off, and they lay there quietly, listening to the faint sucking
noises of the water and the dull traffic noises of the city, seven
or eight miles away, saying nothing, looking straight up at the
stars.

'Mike . . .'

'Yeah?'

'What were you thinking?'

'Nothing . . .'

'You must have been thinking something –'

'You won't laugh?'

'No.'

'I was thinking of Ezra Pound.'

'Who's he?'

'A poet. He's the poet who listens to water running and then
tries to put the sounds into words.'

'Oh . . .'

They were silent again. April moved her head over and kissed his breast, making a little noise of relaxed contentment in her throat.

'Mike . . .'

'Yeah?'

'Do you love me?'

'I don't know. I like you, I know that.'

'Well do you love to love me?'

'Yes . . .'

'There won't be many more times like this.'

'I know it – '

'What's going to happen to us?'

'Nothing's going to happen to us – '

'I mean in the future. I mean in years to come.'

'Well, you're going to marry that nice guy from Yale, and settle down and have a family. And then about the time you have a couple of swell kids we'll be in a war and your couple of swell kids'll be wiped out with enemy gas or bombs or something. And I'll be lying like this on some foreign battlefield, only I'll have shrapnel in my belly, and the vultures will be eating me.'

'You don't really think that?'

'Yes, I do. We're getting ready for it. A lot of stupid sonsabitches are rushing us into it head first. Mussolini started it and then came Hitler. Mussolini told Great Britain to kiss his arse and made them like it. The League of Nations is yellow. And Japan is around the corner, waiting with a blackjack – '

'I don't think this country will go to war. People are against it.'

'They are until we get in it. When they start playing the national anthem and waving a flag, everybody gets hysterical.'

She reached over and took his hand, moving her head a little closer, so close he could smell the oil in her hair. He raised himself up on his elbow, looking down at her. She was a length of curving white against the dark blue and red tartan. She

moaned, wanting him again. He leaned down and took her in
his arms.

'Mike,' she said, between her teeth, 'if you do have to go to
war there's one thing that must not happen to you. Oh, God,
anything but that . . .'

At ten o'clock the following morning Dolan was at the theatre
waiting for David, sitting in the reception-room upstairs, looking at a magazine, fingering the pages, none of it registering on
his mind, because he was thinking about the fifteen hundred
dollars.

'Hello, hello,' the Major said, coming out of his office.
'Well. This is a surprise. Don't you feel well, Dolan?'

'I feel swell,' Dolan said. 'Why?'

'Nothing. Only it's been a long time since you've been
around here this early in the morning.'

'None of the old gang comes around any more,' Dolan said,
laying down the magazine. 'You know why.'

'So that's what's the matter with you. That's what's sticking
in your craw.'

'It's what's sticking in everybody else's, too. There's too much
efficiency around here. Look at this room. Look at the rug.
God, this joint's a palace now. It's not like the old barn we had.'

'This is the finest Little Theatre in the country,' the Major
said, a little proudly.

'That's exactly what I'm talking about,' Dolan said. 'It is the
finest – that's the trouble with it. Only it's not a Little Theatre
– not strictly. It's professional now.'

'Not professional – semi-professional.'

'It's the same damned thing. You know, Major, winning those
tournaments in New York was the worst thing that ever
happened to us.'

'Why? Why do you say a thing like that? You ought to be
ashamed of yourself. You were one of the organizers of the
Little Theatre in this town.'

'That's why I'm not ashamed to say it. We used to play in a barn, didn't we? A little lousy barn with benches for seats and no dressing-rooms. We did Dostoevsky and Ibsen and some plays by farmer boys who live around here – '

'Those local plays were very bad – '

'What if they were? By God, we gave 'em some sort of production! We encouraged the writers. How do you know we mightn't have unearthed another O'Neill or Shaw? We had no overhead, and we could use local people in the cast, green people. There might have been another Bernhardt or Duse or Irving in them.'

'We use local people now, don't we?'

'A few – but it's more of a stock company. We've got to use experienced casts, and we've got to do hit plays, because we've got a mortgage to meet. What the hell are we doing for local talent? Nothing.'

'I'm surprised to hear you talk like that, Dolan. I thought you, of all people, were grateful for what the Chamber of Commerce has done.'

'Grateful!' Dolan exclaimed, getting up, walking around. 'I'm not in the least grateful. I loathe and despise 'em, the bastards. When we were in the old barn, I went to 'em time after time to try to get some money. They wouldn't give us a nickel. They thought I was crazy. You know how I raised the money to get into that first tournament in New York don't you?'

'I know, but – '

'You're goddam right, you know. I canvassed this town from Weston Park to the river, getting two bucks here and a buck there and four-bits from somebody else. And we won the lousy tournament. And we went back and won two more. And then what happened? The Chamber of Commerce decided to cash in on us. They got the Kiwanians and the Rotarians and the rest of those goddam luncheon clubs together, and the first thing you know we're out here in a hundred-and-fifty-thousand dollar Little Theatre, this great Greek-Byzantine-Gothic-Mayan-

Moroccan Temple of Art. Now it's an institution with expenses
to meet; out the back door goes everything all of the old gang
ever worked for and in the front door come all the goddam club
women and their cheap politics and all the lesbians and homosexuals in town. That's what's sticking in my craw. The
Chamber of Commerce!'

'I'm sorry you feel that way, Dolan, truly I am,' the Major
said, taking his arm. 'You're a leader around here. I'd counted
on you to help me.'

'I've got nothing against you, Major,' Dolan said. 'Hell, you
couldn't help it. You're a marvellous director. When they got
this magnificent theatre, they had to get a paid director to go
with it – somebody with a national reputation. It was too big a
job for us. I'm not sore at you.'

'I want you to know I'm your friend – '

'I'm your friend, too, Major. The way I feel has got nothing
to do with you. It's the theatre. It's that goddam Chamber of
Commerce. Why couldn't they have let us alone?'

'Don't blame them – they only did what they thought was
right. I'm sorry you feel this way, Dolan, truly I am,' he said
again. 'You could be a terrific force for good if you'd only
try. Underneath this hard-boiled shell of yours you're a nice
kid – '

'Don't start that again, Major. What the hell!'

'All right, Dolan,' he said, plainly aggrieved. 'I'm only trying
to help you find a little happiness – '

' – Morning,' David said, coming in from the steps. 'Sorry
I'm late.'

'Hello,' Dolan said slowly, ill-at-ease, wondering how much
of the conversation David had overheard.

'See you tonight, Dolan,' the Major said, going abruptly into
his office.

'What's the matter with him?' David asked.

'Nothing. You know the Major. Giving me another fight
talk.'

'I ought to give you a fight talk, too,' David said, looking at him slyly. 'I called you around three o'clock this morning, and Larry said you were still out.'

'Oh,' Dolan said. 'Yeah.'

'Come on in,' David said, taking off his hat, going through a door.

'I like this office better than I do the Major's,' Dolan said.

'It's much smaller,' David said, throwing his hat on the davenport, crossing to the desk, and sitting down.

'That's why I like it. Hell, when I think about the old barn – we had an office a little bigger than a dry-goods box, and at night we had to use it for a dressing-room.'

'I've heard plenty about that old barn. Must have been fun.'

'It was. Say, those are new, aren't they?' Dolan asked suddenly, pointing to the wall.

'Yes. I painted those.'

'You did?' Dolan exclaimed, moving over, looking at them. 'They're nice. I didn't know you went in for water-colours.'

'I didn't know you went in for art,' David said, smiling.

'I have to in self-defence,' Dolan said, laughing. 'I live with four painters, a budding young writer, and a German war ace. They sit up all night talking about it.'

'That's an interesting group over there.'

'I don't know how interesting it is, but I guess we've got a lot in common. Look, David, I don't want to be rude, but – '

'But you want the cheque, huh?'

'Well – '

'Sit down, Mike – '

'I hope you haven't changed your mind about letting me have it,' Dolan said, sitting down, wondering what was coming.

'I haven't changed my mind. I'm just curious to know if you realize what you're getting into.'

'Getting into?'

'Johnny told me all about it last night. When you were rehearsing. I'd hate to see you make a mistake.'

'I'll pay you back – '

'It's not that I'm thinking of. It's your magazine. I wouldn't like to see you get into trouble.'

'I'm not going to get into trouble,' Dolan said shortly.

'You're going to try to tell the truth, aren't you?'

'I'm not going to try to, I'm going to do it.'

'Have you stopped to think what might happen if you stepped on the wrong toes? This is an overgrown country town, filled with narrow-minded people, bigots – and they'll resent anybody who makes an effort to change conditions, I know. I know what towns like this are like.'

'I know too. I was born here.'

'They'll crucify you – '

'Look, David, for God's sake, don't lecture me. Everybody is always lecturing to me. I know what I'm doing – do I get the money or not?' he said, standing up, biting his lip.

'. . . All right,' David said finally, opening the drawer, taking out his cheque-book.

Lawrence met him as he came in the door of the printing plant and took him upstairs to a vacant office.

'I think you'll find this room satisfactory,' he said. 'I'll have it cleaned out for you in the morning. We've been using it as a storeroom for our layouts and art work.'

'This'll do fine,' Dolan said. 'All I need is a desk and a typewriter, and what about a key to the place?'

'I'll have a key made for you,' Lawrence said. 'I want you to have a talk with Mr Eckman about the advertising. Eckman handles the advertising for several of the house organs we print. He'll handle yours. Just make yourself at home,' Lawrence said, going out.

'When do you plan to put out the first issue, Dolan?' Eckman said.

'In about a week – '

'Got anybody in mind who might throw us some business?'

'Not right now I haven't. I hadn't given that angle much thought.'

'It's rather an important angle. Got to have business to pay the freight, you know – '

'I know.'

'What about your friends? You ought to have some friends in some of the stores who could give us an account.'

'I haven't,' Dolan said. 'I'm sorry. I'm pretty new to this racket, but I'll try to think up some prospects for you.'

'Well, in the meantime I'll make the usual rounds,' Eckman said. 'Have you decided on a name for the magazine yet?'

'I think I'll call it the *Cosmopolite*.'

'The *Cosmopolite*! Not bad,' Eckman said. 'Not bad.'

'Do you think you can get any business for the first issue?'

'I don't see why we can't get some,' Eckman said, moving towards the door. 'Of course, the advertising business is always tough, but the novelty of this ought to get us some.'

'It certainly will be a help if we can,' Dolan said.

'I'll give it a whirl,' Eckman said, smiling. 'Well, so long – '

'So long,' Dolan said, looking out the window into the street below . . .

'Good afternoon,' Myra's voice said.

'Hello!' Dolan said, turning, surprised that he had not heard her come in.

'How are you?'

'Fine . . . all right.'

'Well,' she said, smiling, 'aren't you going to ask me to sit down?'

'Sure – excuse me,' Dolan said, coming around and getting a chair for her. 'There you are – '

'Thanks . . . What's the matter with your face?'

'Oh,' he said, rubbing the short beard, 'I didn't feel like shaving this morning – '

'I don't mean that,' Myra said, shaking her head. 'I mean

that –' she leaned over and touched his cheek with her finger. 'Right there.'

'It's a bruise, I guess. I must have hit something.'

'Looks like a bite,' Myra said. 'You don't go around letting women bite you, do you?'

Dolan flushed, feeling a little uncomfortable . . .

'Nice place you've got here,' Myra said, looking around. 'Is that my desk over there?'

'Your desk?'

'Yes. I'm going to help you, you know – '

'I don't need any help.'

'You'll need plenty before you get through with this,' she said, with conviction. 'I don't think you realize quite what you're up against.'

'It's not as bad as that,' he said, smiling. 'Anyway, I'm not in a position to put anybody to work. I told you that yesterday. I haven't got any money. I intend to do all the writing myself.'

'Travelling on your nerve?'

'In a way – '

'And your hatreds?'

'Oh, I don't have any hatreds – '

'That's the nicest thing about you,' she said, smiling, parting those red, red lips. 'You do have. Keep 'em. Keep 'em alive. They'll be very useful to you.'

'Who are you?' Dolan asked abruptly, beginning to feel like shivering again.

'Why, I'm Myra – ' she said.

'I know you're Myra. Where'd you come from?'

'New York. I've been here a couple of months.'

'Where'd you meet Bishop?'

'I met him here. I had a letter to him from a friend of his in New York. That's how I met him. Why are you so curious?'

'I'm damned if I know,' Dolan said, looking out the window. 'I've never been curious about women before. Usually I take 'em or leave 'em and ask no questions. But this is different. It's damned funny about you and me,' he said, turning back to look at her. 'Goddam funny.'

'So you've finally realized that?'

'I knew it yesterday when I first met you. You know what's been going through my mind off and on since then?'

'Certainly I know. You've been wondering about that cup of coffee I missed – and just what bearing that's going to have on your future.'

'That's it exactly,' Dolan said, no longer surprised to hear her put his own thoughts into words.

'Something like that's been going through my mind, too,' Myra said. 'Yesterday I thought it was strange, but that was because under the impact of first meeting you I didn't stop to think about it. We think it's strange, because we don't understand it. Look. A man stops to buy a newspaper in the lobby of his office building. This particular man has never bought a paper here before. On the way to his office he has passed dozens of newsboys with that same paper for sale. He didn't buy one then. But in the lobby of the building, for no explainable reason, he *does* buy one. In that second he misses the elevator. In that elevator is a woman who would have been his wife – or a business friend who would have tipped him off to a million-dollar deal. Or – the elevator falls and kills everybody in it. But *this man* paused to buy a paper – something he had never done before. Do you understand why he did it?'

'No,' Dolan said; 'not exactly.'

'Well, that's what happened to us. I did *not* stop to get my *usual* cup of coffee – '

'I just wonder,' Dolan said, 'whether that's going to be bad for you and good for me or bad for me and good for you – '

'I wonder too . . .' Myra said. 'At any rate, I'm going along with you. What time shall I come down in the morning?'

'But – '

'What time will you be here?'

'Around nine, but – '

'I'll see you then, Michael Dolan,' she said, getting up, going out, not looking back . . .

Dolan worked until late that afternoon, planning his new magazine, thinking up new titles for the various departments, writing stuff for 'The Main Stem', which was almost identical in style with 'The Talk of the Town' in the *New Yorker*; but the thought of Myra Barnovsky kept popping in and out of his mind, and he could not be clever no matter how desperately he tried, and he would think of her red, red lips, and then he would make a mistake and would go to his typewriter, and then he would curse because he hated dirty copy, and if he made a single mistake on a page he would take it out and start all over again, and finally it was late in the afternoon and he gave up, thinking he would be down in the morning and get a good start; he would go home to the house and take a nap, because he and April had had a hell of a night out in the country on the banks of a brook with their clothes off in the moonlight, and he hadn't got much sleep.

'This'll wear off,' he said to himself, going down to get in his car, thinking of Myra. 'By tomorrow I'll be used to this dame, and then I can settle down to work.'

He drove home, to the big three-storey house he shared with the four young painters, the would-be writer, and the German war ace, and went upstairs and slept an hour. It was a peaceful hour in which he dreamed of absolutely nothing. When he waked up it was dark. He turned on the light and went in the bathroom – and came promptly out, swearing.

'Hey, Ulysses,' he yelled. 'Ulysses! Goddam it!'

'Yes, sir, Mister Mike,' Ulysses called, coming up the back stairs. He was the Negro major-domo of the house.

'What the hell about that?' Dolan asked, pointing to the toilet bowl on which was propped a small framed canvas with 'OUT OF ORDER' printed on the back of it.

'Mister Elbert stuck that up there,' Ulysses said. 'That's one of his old oils.'

'I don't mean the painting. I mean the bowl. Why the hell hasn't it been fixed? Why didn't you call Mrs Ratcliff?'

'I did, Mister Mike. She said she didn't mind us all artists living here without paying rent, but that she wasn't going to fix no plumbing till she collected some money from us.'

'Hell,' Dolan said. 'I'll go downstairs. Bring my shaving stuff, will you?'

'Yes, sir. And, Mister Mike, would you mind if I picked out one of your ties to wear tonight?'

'I guess not, Ulysses. I guess if we can't pay you your twenty dollars a month we can at least let you wear our ties. It's too bad you're such a little buck that you can't wear my clothes.'

'That's all right, Mister Mike. Mister Elbert let me have one of his suits and Mister Walter loaned me his car – '

'Is his gas tank empty again?'

'Yes, sir. I promised to put in five gallons.'

'Ulysses, he's taking advantage of your reputation as a great lover. Hot stuff, tonight, huh?'

'Yes, sir,' Ulysses said, grinning, getting the shaving stuff out of the medicine cabinet.

'You take any tie you want, Casanova. And get me a clean pair of socks, will you? I'll take a shower downstairs,' Dolan said, going out, downstairs to the ground floor.

'Ulysses upstairs?' Tommy Thornton, one of the artists, asked, as Dolan went through the living-room.

'Yeah. He'll be down in a minute.'

'Goddam coon. He piled all the dishes in the sink and left them.'

'He's got a date.'

'He's always got a date. He hangs on the phone all day long talking to those high yellows. I'm getting sick and tired of it.'

'Somebody better use it while the using's good. We won't have it much longer,' Dolan said, going on to the bathroom.

'Come on in,' Walter said, looking around, drying his hands.

'Goddam bathroom upstairs is still out of order,' Dolan said. 'Ratcliff won't fix it until we pay the rent.'

'So Ulysses was telling me.'

'Can't say as I blame the old dame much. She's been pretty nice so far.'

'I might be able to do something about it tomorrow. I think I've got a painting sold.'

'I hope so, Walter. A couple of sales under your belt and you'll be a new man. Put the stuff down there, Ulysses.'

'Yes, sir,' Ulysses said, putting the socks and the shaving stuff in a chair. 'Anything else I can do for you?'

'That's all – '

'Anything you want, Mister Walter?'

'No, thanks – '

'Good night,' Ulysses said, backing out.

'Goddam good nigger,' Walter said.

'The best,' Dolan said. 'He'd go to hell for any one of us. Except Tommy. Tommy's a snob. Can he paint?'

'He could if he'd work. He won't work.'

'He thinks he's a genius, that's why. He wants to sit on his ass and have fame come up and lay her head in his lap,' Dolan said, taking off his clothes.

'And you seem to be doing all right with your women, too,' Walter said. 'I heard you come in this morning with the milkman.'

'Yeah,' Dolan said. 'But this afternoon I was with the most interesting girl I've ever met – '

'Where have I heard that before?' Walter said, laughing.

'I mean it,' Dolan said. 'Sort of olive complexion, black eyes, black hair, and the reddest goddam lips you ever saw. One of those cruel types. Looks like a sadist.'

'Sounds mysterious.'

'It is mysterious,' Dolan said, lathering his face. 'I've always been a sucker for mystery anyway. The trouble with me is

I'm too goddam dramatic. Everything that happens to me is a situation.'

'Maybe you're a genius too,' Walter said. 'Wouldn't it be funny if we were *all* geniuses?'

'I guess we're on the way, at that. Plumbing is out of order, and we can't pay the rent. That's usually a prerequisite.'

'Mike,' Tommy said, sticking his head in the door, 'there's a lady out here to see you.'

'A lady?' Dolan asked, turning round. 'Who?'

'She said her name was Marsden – '

'Mary Margaret?' Dolan asked.

'Her mother,' Tommy replied.

'I haven't got time to talk to her now,' Dolan said, frowning. 'I've got to shave and bathe and get to rehearsal.'

'I told her that, but she wouldn't take no for an answer.'

'Okay,' Dolan said heavily, putting down the shaving brush, wiping the lather off his face.

'I thought you were finished with Mary Margaret,' Walter said.

'I am. I haven't seen her in a couple of weeks. Except for that thing the other morning.'

'That's pretty good understatement – "that thing",' Walter said. 'She fell in the front door at three o'clock screaming for you.'

'She was drunk,' Dolan said, putting on his shirt.

'She was raising enough hell so's you could hear her in Weston Park. What do you do to 'em, Mike?'

'Search me,' Dolan said. 'I'm just plain hoodooed, I guess. Every dame that falls for me is a nymph. Well, kid, stand by for emergencies,' he said, starting out.

'Mike – can you spare me a fin?'

'I wish I could, Walter,' Dolan said. 'I haven't got that much.'

'Okay. I wouldn't have mentioned it except I thought you got paid when you quit the paper.'

'I only had one day's salary coming. I told the cashier to buy Brandon a new pair of shoes with it.'

'Brandon? Who's Brandon?'

'Don't you know Brandon? Head of the Community Chest. Well, if I yell, come a-running,' Dolan said, going out. 'Where is she?' he asked Tommy.

'Upstairs. Good luck, Casanova.'

'You got me mixed up with Ulysses,' Mike said, going upstairs.

Mrs Marsden was sitting on the davenport, straight-backed, staring at the African Gold Coast fetishes on the mantel when Dolan came down to her.

'Hello, Mrs Marsden,' he said.

'Good evening, Mr Dolan,' Mrs Marsden said evenly. 'I wanted to speak to you about Mary Margaret.'

'What about Mary Margaret?' Dolan asked, sitting down on the davenport.

'I've sent her away,' Mrs Marsden said, 'and I've come to ask you not to answer any of her letters.'

'Oh,' Dolan said, relieved. 'I won't. I didn't even know she had gone away.'

'Last week. I finally decided it was best. Since Mr Marsden died I've had the responsibility of Mary Margaret alone, and I finally decided to send her to my sister's in Mexico City. She's so young and innocent, you know – '

'Yes, I know,' Dolan said. 'Well, Mrs Marsden, you could have saved yourself a trip. I promise you I won't answer any of her letters. What made you think she'd write to me after what happened?'

'Now, don't insult my intelligence. I know the girl was fond of you – '

'Not any more,' Dolan said. 'You broke that up. I'd like to ask you a question, Mrs Marsden. What have you got against me?'

'In the first place, Mr Dolan, I don't like men who take money from young girls – '

'What makes you think I took her money?'

'I saw the cancelled cheques. Several hundred dollars' worth.'

'That's right,' Dolan said. 'I didn't think you knew. But I paid her back a hundred dollars. I'll pay the rest as soon as I get it.'

'My, my,' Mrs Marsden said, leaning a little closer to him, shaking her head. 'These young girls! You've cut quite a swath among them, haven't you?'

'I hadn't thought of it that way,' he replied, looking at the clock. 'Well, Mrs Marsden . . .'

'I don't wonder they lose their heads,' Mrs Marsden said, not taking the hint. 'This Bohemian house and all its old furniture and old paintings – '

'Yes. Well –' Dolan said, standing up.

'And its fascinating literature,' she said, picking up a book from the coffee-table, holding it up. 'I was glancing through this while I was waiting for you. Did you write it?'

'No,' Dolan said, blushing in spite of himself. 'I don't know how that got out here.'

'And such illustrations! This is the first erotica I've seen in years.'

'I don't know how it got out here. I usually keep it in the bookcase in my room.'

'Where is your room?' Mrs Marsden asked, standing up, holding the book in front of her.

'Right in there,' Dolan said, pointing. 'That's my room.'

'I'll put this away with my own hands,' Mrs Marsden said, going across the floor. 'It's dangerous to leave books like this lying around.'

'I'm sorry I have to rush off, Mrs Marsden,' Dolan said, following her inside the room. 'But I'm late for rehearsal now,' he said, reaching for the light switch.

'Don't turn that on,' Mrs Marsden whispered, her hot breath in his ear. 'Don't . . .'

'Well, I'll be a son of a bitch,' Dolan said to himself.

*

It was after eight o'clock when he got to the Little Theatre and
started down the aisle to the stage.

'Wait! Wait a minute up there!' the Major yelled to the
players on stage, stopping the rehearsal, then turning to glare at
Dolan. 'How much longer is this going to keep up?' he asked
angrily.

'I'm sorry, Major; I couldn't help it,' Dolan said contritely.

'Do you think we're running this theatre for your special
benefit? . . . Do you? Answer me?'

'I've told you I was sorry,' Dolan said nervously, aware that
the cast was looking at him over the footlights.

'You've got to cut this out! I only wish,' the Major said,
turning to David and a couple of others from the production
staff who sat with him in the auditorium, 'that we hadn't already
announced the production. If it hadn't gone this far I'd chuck
the whole business. Apologize to the cast, Dolan.'

'But, Major – '

'You've never shown the slightest consideration for the
people in this cast: you've been rude and impolite and arrogant,
acting as if you were the producer, writer, director, and star of
every production. I've told you before that nobody in this
theatre is any more important than anybody else.'

'I didn't mean to be rude, Major,' Dolan said in level tone.
'I'm sorry I'm always late. I don't seem to be able to help it.'

'Apologize!'

'. . . I'm sorry, everybody,' Dolan said finally, to the players
on the stage. 'I'll not let this happen again. Was that satisfactory?' he asked the Major.

'Yes. Timothy's been pinch-hitting for you. All right, Timothy,'
he called. 'Come on down. Dolan'll carry on.'

'You stay right where you are, Timothy,' Dolan said.

'You've been an understudy around here long enough. I quit,'
he said to the Major, walking up the aisle, through the lobby
into the night.

*

'Dolan! Dolan!' the Major called from the top of the stairs, walking rapidly down them to the car at the kerb. 'Just a minute – '

'It's all right, Major,' Dolan said, turning the ignition key off. 'No hard feelings – '

'But we open next week – '

'Let Timothy have the part. He's worked his head off for years. Give him a break.'

'Dolan – you can't leave me in a hole like this – '

'You'd be in a worse hole if I stayed. I'm no good, Major – it's best this way. Anyway, since rehearsals began things have changed for me and I won't have time to fool with the theatre.'

'I didn't mean to embarrass you in there – '

'Don't let's both be dam' fools, Major,' Dolan said quietly. 'I had it coming. I guess I was rude. I just never thought of it that way before.'

'But – you need the theatre badly. You need what it can give you. Won't you please – for my sake?' the Major asked, ducking down, putting his head inside the car, under the top.

'Look out, Major – I'm going,' Dolan said huskily, turning the ignition key, starting the motor. 'If I don't go now I'll never go,' he said, letting in the clutch, rolling away.

2

THE first issue of the *Cosmopolite* was delivered to the news-stands the following Wednesday afternoon, and as Dolan was climbing the stairs to his office on Thursday morning he met Eddie Bishop coming down.

'Well, you son of a bitch,' Bishop said gaily, sticking out his hand. 'You did it!'

'Did you see it?' Dolan asked, shaking hands.

'Did I see it? Everybody on the paper saw it.'

'Come on in,' Dolan said, steering him into the office. 'Myra, here's that goddam Communist. I couldn't have put out the magazine without Myra's help.'

'Hello, Ed,' Myra said. 'Several people called,' she said to Dolan. 'There's the list on your desk.'

'I went around the news-stands this morning to check on the sales. That's why I'm late.'

'How's it going?' Bishop asked, sitting down.

'All right. I don't know much about these things. I guess it's going all right. Tell me, Ed – on the level now – what did you think?'

'I thought it was swell, Mike. Truthfully. But it's a lot like the *New Yorker*, isn't it?'

'Any magazine this type's got to be like the *New Yorker*. Except for the society stuff.'

'That's the only part I didn't like. That society section.'

'Got to have a society section – and the débutantes' pictures. Pretty good raft of advertising too, wasn't it?'

'Who got that? You?'

'Guy named Eckman. Works for Lawrence. Did Thomas

see that stuff about the baseball team?'

'I think he bought the first issue. I picked one up about four o'clock and took it in to him – and he had already finished reading it.'

'What'd he say?'

'He didn't mind the baseball exposé as much as he did that editorial about the newspapers being muzzled by the advertising departments. That made him blow his topper.'

'Well, it's the truth,' Dolan said.

'Sure, it's the truth,' Bishop said. 'Look, Mike – you don't have to tell me. Don't I know goddam well it's the truth! You're not the only reporter who ever ran up against that in a newspaper. We all do.'

' "Freedom of the press",' Dolan said sarcastically. 'God, what a laugh!'

'I'm going to tell you one thing, kid,' Bishop said. 'I'm damned afraid you're bumping your head against a stone wall. You're going to make a lot of enemies. A lot of people are going to hate your guts for this. Thomas, for instance. You know what he's doing in the afternoon edition? He's writing an editorial on the sport page answering your charges about the dear old *Times-Gazette* being censored and suppressed.'

'I hope he does. I hope to hell he does. I've got him nailed to the cross and he knows it. Besides,' Dolan said, grinning, 'it'll be swell exploitation for the magazine. It'll make people buy it.'

'A lot of stupid goddam yokels who won't believe what you say – '

'I'll make 'em believe it!' Dolan said, a little fiercely. 'By God, I'll give 'em dates and figures and names. I'll give 'em affidavits. That baseball business is only the beginning. I'm going right up from the bottom, through the city hall, and the District Attorney's office, and into the Governor's mansion – '

'If you last that long.'

'Oh, I'll last that long,' Dolan said.

'I'll lay you a bet that if you go through with this idea they'll have this place closed up so tight in six months you can't get in with a truck-load of T.N.T.'

'Over my dead body,' Dolan said.

'All right – you'll see. But, hell, don't get me wrong. I'm for you. Why do you think I came up here to see you?'

'Why?'

'Well . . . I've been on police run for fifteen years, and I've seen some pretty raw things happen. Any time you want an article done, I'll do it. I couldn't afford to have my name signed to it, you understand – on account of the wife and kids – but I'll do it anonymously.'

'Thanks, Ed, but I'm through with anonymous stuff. There'll be a name signed to anything I print that looks dangerous. Tell you what you might do, though. You might give me a tip once in a while. I haven't any budget yet, but I'll pay you sometime – '

' – Hello, Dolan,' a voice drawled from the doorway.

'Oh, hello, Mr Thomas,' Dolan said, looking up. 'Come in – '

'Hi, Tommy – ' Bishop mumbled.

'Who are you working for – me or him?' Thomas asked, finally noticing him.

'Why – you, Tommy. I just dropped in – '

'Well, just drop out. Or don't you give a damn what goes on at police headquarters?'

'Okay,' Bishop said, getting up, looking daggers at Thomas. 'See you around, Mike – '

'Good-bye, Eddie,' Myra said, still typing.

'So long, Myra – '

'Sit down, Mr Thomas,' Dolan said.

'I think better on my feet,' Thomas said gruffly. 'What's the idea of blasting at me?'

'I wasn't blasting at you. I was blasting at all the newspapers.'

'But everybody in town knows you worked for the *Times-*

Gazette, and they'll know you meant us.'

'That's drawing a pretty fine line – '

'That story about the baseball scandal has gone over both press wires. You've kicked up a hell of a stink. You'll probably hear from Landis.'

'I hope so – that was the idea.'

'Well – I'm interested first of all in the *Times-Gazette*. I won't stand for you attacking us with vicious editorials.'

'What you're really afraid of,' Dolan said, 'is that you'll be shown up. You and the other three papers.'

'We'll make it goddam tough for you if you don't lay off. I'm telling you.'

'Why, for God's sake, I've only begun. You wait until I really get into action,' he said, pulling a sheet of paper out of his inside pocket. 'These are some notes I've made in the past few days of stories to write – stories the papers should have written months ago. "Dr Carlisle," ' he read. 'You know him, the eminent abortionist, who already has killed a couple of girls and who still is permitted to carry on his wholesale business because his brother is the boss of Colton county. "Carson." The Supervisor of Streets who gets a rakeoff on all trucks sold to the city. "Riccarcelli." The guy who has a gambling-house in the biggest hotel in town. "Nestor." The Police Commissioner, a farmer boy six years ago and who now rides in a Deusenberg. That'll give you a rough idea of what's on the surface. God knows what I'll find when I start digging.'

'There's nothing new about any of that,' Thomas said. 'Every town in the country has the same thing to put up with. It's part of the recognized system. You're absolutely insane if you touch any of those stories.'

'Touch 'em! I'm going to milk 'em. I'm going to give that erudite Grand Jury something to do.'

'You're going to commit suicide, that's what you're going to do. Go ahead if you want to – but remember this, don't print any more vicious editorials about the *Times-Gazette* or I'll settle with you personally,' Thomas said, walking out, banging his heels on the floor.

'Sociable fellow,' Myra said, stopping her typing. 'I hope you don't let him bluff you.'

'I'm scared to death,' Dolan said, grinning.

'Have you seen that list of calls? A couple of them said it was important – Miss Coughlin and a Mrs Marsden. A Mr Cookson also called. Said it was urgent – '

'That's the Major. The Little Theatre director.' The telephone rang.

'Hello . . .' Myra said. 'Yes, this is Beachwood 4556 . . . Chicago? Who's calling? . . . All right, operator, put them on – '

'Who is it?' Dolan asked, frowning, taking the telephone.

'It's from a gentleman who has something or other to do with baseball. I believe she said his name was Landis . . .'

LANDIS OUTLAWS SIX COLTON

PLAYERS

CONVICTED OF ACCEPTING BRIBES IN

CHAMPIONSHIP SERIES

By Humphrey Presnell

Six first-string members of the Colton baseball team were today outlawed from organized baseball by Commissioner Kenesaw Mountain Landis for accepting bribes to lose the series with Benntown, which determined the 1936 pennant. The players have been on trial five days.

Their names are Fritz Dockstetter, pitcher; Harold Mullock, second baseman; Joe Trent, outfielder and league's leading batsman; Raoul Deadrick, outfielder; Mercer Castle, first baseman; and Adrian Potts, catcher.

It was understood that two of the players had made a full confession to Commissioner Landis without revealing the source of the bribe. None of them would make a statement to the *Evening Courier*.

Attention was first directed to the scandal by the *Cosmopolite*, month-old weekly magazine, edited by Michael Dolan, former sports editor of a local paper . . .

'I must say Presnell did all right by us,' Dolan said, folding the newspaper. 'All over page one.'

'It's a big story,' Myra said. 'It's in every newspaper in the country.'

'I'm tickled to death they got kicked out,' Dolan said. 'The bastards. I like Landis. No red tape with him. He'll keep baseball clean. It's too bad politics hasn't got a Landis. By God, how they need one! One Landis in politics would do this country more good than six Supreme Courts.'

'Hell!' Ed Bishop said suddenly. 'Listen to this editorial in the *Times-Gazette*: "The *Times-Gazette* joins with every lover of clean sport in wishing the six crooked Colton baseball players a speedy trip to Limbo – " '

'Thomas wrote that,' Dolan said. ' "Speedy trip to Limbo." Ugh! Go ahead – '

' "They were the idols of the youngsters in this city – and probably others in the circuit – but they were unfaithful to their trusts, and now they are for ever barred from organized baseball. Splendid. Whatever part we have played in the unmasking of these betrayers is but further indication that the *Times-Gazette* will not tolerate corruption of public office or of public men or of – baseball players." Is that a laugh or not?' he asked, grinning.

'I expected that,' Dolan said. 'All that editorial needs to make it a perfect example of how not to write is for it to have a one-line head: "Crime Does Not Pay." '

'It's got it,' Bishop said. 'So help me, it's got it! Look! "Crime Does Not Pay." '

'Well, I'll be a son of a bitch,' Dolan exclaimed, looking at the paper Bishop held, verifying it. 'Isn't that marvellous? You know something, Ed? You're lucky Thomas canned you. I'd rather starve to death and write what I wanted to than to work for that lousy *Times-Gazette*.'

'So had I,' Bishop said dryly. 'At least that's what I'm doing. I'd just got a raise to fifty-five a few days before Thomas came up here and caught me in the office. You're paying me twenty-five. Of course, the real reason he canned me was because he saw me here that day and thought we were cooking up something. Me getting scooped when that tart got shot, wasn't it. Hell, that's only a one-paragraph story. He just used that as an excuse.'

'Hello, Dolan – Hello, Myra,' Lawrence said breezily, coming into the office.

'This is Mr Bishop, Mr Lawrence. Late of the distinguished *Times-Gazette*.'

'How do you do, Mr Bishop,' Lawrence said, shaking hands.

'I put Bishop to work yesterday,' Dolan said.

'You did?' Lawrence exclaimed.

'I got him fired, so I put him to work. Myra and I can't do it all. Ed's a goddam good man. Got guts. What's that in your hand?'

'The new circulation report. I wanted you to see it.'

'Thanks,' Dolan said, taking it. 'Did Eckman have any luck today?'

'He hasn't come in yet, but I think we'll do all right now.'

'We ought to do better than all right with everybody in town talking about the *Cosmopolite*,' Dolan said, glancing at the circulation figures. 'Three thousand, one-one-one. Not bad for the fourth week. We ought to get plenty of advertisers now.'

'I hope we do,' Lawrence said. 'Three thousand circulation at ten cents each isn't much. Are you working tonight?'

'We've checked the page proofs and they're ready to be set up. Nothing we can do tonight.'

'How're the subscriptions coming, Myra?'

'Fair. I've called about a hundred people on the list and got about twenty annuals.'

'Well, keep after them,' Lawrence said, going out.

'I don't think that guy likes me,' Bishop said.

'Sure, he does. He's a little tight with his money, that's all.'

'What'd he mean about three thousand circulation at ten cents a copy? That's not all the income, is it? What about those ads?'

'Well, Eddie, don't let this go any farther – but most of those ads were give-aways. We donated those to the stores to prove we could pull business.'

'Then where are you going to get the money to pay me?' Bishop asked, puzzled.

'I think we're going to get it out of the magazine, but don't worry about it. In case everything else fails, I've got a private gold mine hidden away. Haven't I, Myra?'

'Oh yes, indeed,' Myra said. 'A fifty-five-year-old gold mine.'

A man suddenly stepped through the open door into the office and stood there staring. He was about thirty years old, very stocky, very neatly dressed. All of them saw him, and for two or three seconds not a word was spoken and not a person moved.

'What do you want, Fritz?' Dolan finally said quietly.

'You know what I want,' Dockstetter said slowly, not moving. 'You're the one got me kicked out of baseball. You know what I want, you dirty son of a bitch.'

'Now, wait a minute, Fritz,' Dolan said in almost a pleasant tone, casually easing out from behind the desk. 'I don't want any trouble with you.'

'I guess you know what you've done to my career, don't you?'

'I know what you've done to it,' Dolan said, continuing to drift casually towards him. 'I had this story a month ago, but the paper wouldn't print it. I had to quit my job to nail you.'

'Yeah?' Dockstetter said, putting his right hand in his coat pocket.

'Look out!' Bishop yelled.

Dolan leaped forward, swinging a left that struck Dockstetter on the side of the head, staggering him, driving him backward. Dockstetter was poking with his own left, waving it, while frantically trying to get his doubled fist out of his right pocket. Dolan followed him backward, drilling him under the jaw, then lashing him with a right to the face, slamming him into the wall, crumpling him on the floor. Quickly Dolan was on top of him, tugging at that right hand which was still in the pocket. He finally jerked it out and rammed his own hand inside.

'I thought so,' he said, holding up a pistol. 'A thirty-two. I thought this bastard had murder in his eye.'

'You're not bad with your fists, kid,' Bishop said.

'Well!' Myra exclaimed. 'I was scared for a minute.'

'I'm not so good yet myself,' Dolan said. 'Ed – there's some water in the hall. Hurry up so's we can bring him to. Myra, put this pistol in my desk. Hell! Excitement, hunh?'

'This is only the beginning,' Myra said. 'Wait until we really get going – '

Dolan took Myra to a roof-garden that night for dinner.

'It's nice up here, isn't it?' Myra said.

'I suppose so,' Dolan said, sighing, looking out of the window on to the lights of the town below.

'Don't be so depressed,' Myra said, a little gaily. 'You've got everything in the world to be happy about. Everybody in town is talking about you and the magazine. Since we've been sitting here at least twenty people have come by and congratulated you. And you're doing the thing you wanted to do. So what the hell?'

'I wasn't thinking of that,' Dolan said, glancing towards the orchestra stand, to a big table beside it.

'Oh!' Myra said, following his eyes. 'That! – Well, don't be sore at me. When I suggested coming here I didn't know the girl was having a wedding-party. I didn't even know she was married.'

'I'd forgotten it myself,' Dolan said. 'I guess she thinks I'm a heel to rub it in like this.'

'Like what?'

'Like this. Us being here.'

'What's so horrible about that?'

'For God's sake, will you try to understand? I used to go with April. I used to go with that crowd at her table. Everybody knows I was nuts about her.'

'And that she was nuts about you – '

'At any rate, here I am in the same roof-garden with her wedding-party – and with another girl.'

'A strange girl,' Myra said, wetting her lips. 'A girl nobody knows. A tramp.'

'Now, why the hell act like that?'

'How else do you think I could act? You've just got through telling me you're conspicuous because you're here with a girl who doesn't belong to that crowd – that phoney bunch of so-called upper crust – '

'I didn't say any such thing. You're nuts.'

'You're nuts yourself. For God's sake, why do you care what they think? Why do you keep trying to crash the social register? You're a nobody to them – '

'I know it,' Dolan said soberly.

'They rejected you for every club in town because you were brought up across the tracks. They sneer at you behind your back. They're contemptuous of you. You're a goddam fool, Mike. You've got possibilities, you've got power – and now you're on your way. You're going places. Stop worrying about those cheap little parasites.'

'I'm not worrying as much about them as I am about April. She's a swell egg.'

'The world's full of swell eggs. Are you jealous of the chap who married her – that Menefee?'

'I guess not . . .'

'Then stop being so tragic about it. She's married, and so what? Another lay is out of circulation. From the way you've been moping for the last hour and a half you must think she's the only girl in the world who knows how to fall over.'

'I won't have you saying things like that about April – '

'Oh, God,' Myra said wearily, looking up at the artificial stars in the roof. 'Will you stop being so righteous! I'm only saying what you're thinking – I'm only being honest. Mike,' she said, leaning on her elbows, staring at him, 'I'm only trying to get you to shake this social phobia of yours. Once you get rid of that nothing can stop you. Those people are absolutely worthless. They're just walking around, contributing nothing, taking up a lot of space and breathing a lot of air that could damn well be used by somebody else.'

'I'm not arguing about that,' Dolan said. 'You're probably right. But in spite of everything, they represent something I've never had and something I want very much.'

'You're a frustrated cotillion leader, that's what you are. Let's get the hell out of here.'

'I want to dance a couple of more times . . .'

'You mean you want to dance once with April.'

'Maybe – '

'Well, you go right ahead and make a chump out of yourself,' Myra said, pulling her wrap over her shoulders. 'I'm going.'

'You don't have to, you know – '

'I know I don't have to, but I've got more pride for you than you've got for yourself. I'm going back to your apartment. I'll wait for you there,' she said, standing up.

'I may be pretty late . . .'

'That's all right. I'll get Ulysses to let me into your room. The other boys'll be there. Maybe they can make it interesting for me.'

'You better not in my bed. I'm telling you. I'll slap your ears off.'

'Well, don't be too late then,' she said, moving away.

Dolan got up and threaded his way through the dancing couples to April's table. A hill of flowers swelled from the centre of it. Several chairs were unoccupied.

'Hello, stranger,' April said softly, extending her hand.

'Congratulations,' Dolan said. 'You too, Roy.'

'Thanks,' Menefee said. 'You know these other people, don't you? Harry Carlisle – '

'Sure, I know everybody. Hello!' Dolan said, nodding, sitting down in a chair beside Lillian Fried, a blonde débutante of the year before. 'Hello, Lillian – '

'Hello, Mike – '

'I've got a bone to pick with you, Dolan,' Menefee said. 'You owe me a honeymoon.'

'Yes? How's that?'

'You got April into that Little Theatre show, and now because it's running she can't leave town.'

'I didn't have anything to do with that, Roy. The Major picked her. You're a big hit,' he said to April. 'Swell notices today. How'd it go?'

'Good. You should have been there. We all expected you backstage after the opening – '

'I was pretty busy – '

'You're still a rotten liar, aren't you, Mike?'

'On the level. Magazine's out tomorrow, you know – '

'What about that picture of mine you promised to run?' Lillian said.

'I'll run it next week – '

'Your society page is pretty sick,' Lillian declared. 'Was that your society editor you had over at the table tonight?'

'Not exactly. Why?'

'Nothing – '

'She's a stunning type,' April said. 'Who is she?'

'Oh – she handles the telephones and things – writes a little – '

'I still think I ought to have the job as society editor,' Lillian said. 'I used to work on the school paper – '

'I couldn't pay any money – '

'Oh, I wouldn't want a salary. I'd do it just for the fun of it.'

'What she means,' Harry Carlisle said, leaning over the table, 'is that it would be worth her time just to be around you.'

'Shut up, Harry!' Lillian snapped.

'No offence,' Carlisle said, smiling. 'Just kidding.'

'You're kidding on the square,' Dolan said.

'Would you like to dance, Mike?' April said.

'Well,' Dolan said, asking Menefee the question with his eyes.

'Why not?' Menefee said, standing up, helping April out of her chair.

'Thanks,' Dolan said, getting up, moving with April to the dance floor. 'You suppose this is all right?' he asked, as they started dancing.

'Certainly, silly – '

'I mean, is it ethical to dance with a bride right after she's just become a bride?'

'Certainly. I danced with Roy and Johnny London and Harry Carlisle – '

'Was Johnny here? I didn't see him.'

'You haven't seen anybody. You were too engrossed in that exotic girl you brought. Where is she, by the way?'

'Oh . . . gone.'

'Fight?'

'Sort of – '

'I thought so from your tone. It's too bad. She's damned attractive.'

'It's not serious. We had an argument about coming over to your table. She said not to and . . .'

'I get it. You're still obstinate. Why didn't she want you to come?'

'Oh, no reason. She was right though. They are a lot of snobs. Most of 'em didn't even speak to me. Except Carlisle – and he made a dirty crack.'

'Forget Carlisle. Success has gone to Harry's head. He was telling us tonight he's going to take bigger offices – '

'He ought to. He's got a sure-fire racket – '

'You like Fio Rito?'

'First time I've heard him – in person, I mean. He's all right.'

'Mike . . . why haven't you been around the theatre?'

'Busy.'

'You've never been that busy before. Was it on account of the thing that happened that night – when the Major made you apologize?'

'Not only that. I've really been busy – '

'I've called you a dozen times. Did you get my messages?'

'Yes. I don't like to call you at home, April – you know how the old man feels – and then you were set to marry Roy and everything. You should have let me know. I would have sent a present or something – '

'That's why I called this morning. I wanted to let you know . . .'

'God, this is swell,' Dolan said, holding her a little tighter. 'Say, I wish this thing could have worked out differently – '

'So do I, Mike – '

'God, this is swell,' he said again, feeling the slow movement of her body against his, thinking with a rush of warmth of all the times he had held her.

'Will there ever be any more nights beside our brook, Mike?' she asked in a whisper.

'Good God – yes. Yes – '

'Excuse me,' Menefee said abruptly, thrusting himself between Dolan and April. 'May I finish this one?'

' – All right – ' Dolan said, releasing her. 'Thanks, April. Good night – '

He threaded his way back to his own table and discovered

Carlisle sitting in the chair Myra had vacated.

'Too bad you didn't get to finish your dance,' Carlisle said, smiling. 'I told Menefee to sit still and stop worrying, but he had to go interrupt – '

'That was sweet of you,' Dolan said. 'I know what you mean.'

'Why, from the way you act you'd think I ribbed him to cut in – '

'It doesn't matter,' Dolan said, signalling for the waiter.

'Going?' Carlisle asked.

'Yeah.'

'I was anxious to talk to you – '

'Some other time,' Dolan said, looking at the check, handing the waiter a five-dollar bill.

'Why haven't you ever liked me, Dolan? I like you all right. Why don't you like me?'

'You don't like me, Harry. You didn't like me when we were kids in school and you don't like me now. And I don't like you. I thought you were a prick then, and I think you're a prick now. Just,' – Dolan said, moving his fingers – 'to keep the record straight.'

'And that's why you're going to attack me in your magazine – because you don't like me?'

'What makes you think I'm going to attack you?' Dolan asked, trying to keep the surprise out of his voice.

'Oh – I get around. I just thought I'd remind you that I'm one person in this town you'd better lay off.'

'Don't you think you should wait until I print whatever it is you think I'm going to print before you threaten me?'

'I thought I'd remind you. Just,' – Carlisle said, moving his fingers, imitating Dolan's gesture – 'to keep the records straight.'

' – Thanks,' Dolan said to the waiter, taking the change, giving him a tip. 'Meaning,' he said to Carlisle, 'your brother.'

'Brother? Oh – you mean, Jack. Say,' he said, feigning

surprise, 'that's an idea. Hadn't thought about Jack. Got a lot of power. Maybe I can get him to help me talk you into laying off – '

'Yeah, maybe you can. Maybe he can use some of his power to bring back those three girls you killed performing abortions on 'em – '

Carlisle jumped to his feet. 'Look here, Dolan,' he said, all the oil in his voice suddenly gone, 'you'd goddam well better get your facts straight before you print anything like that!'

'I'll goddam well get 'em straight and you can take a ticket on it,' Dolan said coldly, walking out . . .

There was a light on downstairs when Dolan got home, and through the big windows he could see Elbert and Tommy and Ernst, the ex-war ace, sitting around on the floor with Myra. They were having an earnest discussion of some sort. Dolan went on upstairs to his room and started undressing. He was down to his shorts when Myra came in.

'Don't you ever knock?' he said.

'Here,' she said, grabbing the old bathrobe off a chair, tossing it to him. 'Put this on and everything will be proper.'

'I'm not talking about propriety, I'm talking about politeness. Where the hell are those slippers?' he asked, looking around. 'That goddam Ulysses, I guess he's got 'em down in his room. He's got everything else down there – '

'If you're talking about those awful red moccasins there they are under the desk,' Myra said, pointing. 'I guess you know what time it is, don't you?'

'I took a ride after I left the roof.'

'It must have been a long one. I've been waiting two hours for you – '

'You seemed to be enjoying it,' Dolan said, putting on his slippers. 'What was the subject – that homosexuality is the first law of genius?'

'This time it was about Hitler.'

'That's what I said.'

'Ernst is slightly mad on the subject of pure Aryanism, isn't he?'

'Oh, definitely. That's why he's on the make for all the coloured gals. Ulysses brought his gal here one night and turned his back for a second, and when he turned around she was gone. Ernst had her over on the floor behind the piano. Ulysses was going to carve him up, but we talked him out of it. Oh, definitely Ernst goes for nothing but pure Aryans. And now, Miss Barnovbuttinsky will you get the hell home and let me go to bed?'

'Go ahead to bed. I'm not stopping you.'

'After all, now – '

'I only wanted to talk to you. I can talk as well with you in bed.'

'But I don't want to be talked to,' Dolan said. 'I'm tired of hearing about my complexes and inhibitions and mechanisms. Go home, will you – '

'See April?'

'Yes – '

'How was she taking it?'

'Taking what?'

'Her martyrdom. Being freshly married to the new while still loving the old. That's martyrdom, you know – '

'No kidding,' Dolan said sarcastically.

'Did you get the dance with her?' Myra went on in the same quiet tone.

'About a third of one, yes. Then her husband cut in.'

'Cut in? That was an odd thing to do, wasn't it?'

'He blames me for postponing his honeymoon. He thinks I got April in the Little Theatre show. But Harry Carlisle ribbed him to cut in on me. As I walked away from the table with April I saw Harry move over beside him. Harry reminded him he was supposed to be jealous of me.'

'I'll bet Menefee didn't need much reminding – '

'Hell, that's all over now. When I went back to our table, Carlisle was waiting there for me. He tried to tell me subtly I'd better not print anything about him in the magazine.'

'Oh, that's the Carlisle!'

'That's the one. The famous society doctor.'

'How'd he know you intended printing anything about him?'

'That's what I'd like to find out. Nobody knew about it but you and I and Bishop.'

'And Thomas. Don't forget the day you got sore and tried to impress him by reading the list of people you intended exposing.'

'Yes – and Thomas. Yes.'

'Are Thomas and this Carlisle friends?'

'I don't know. He knows Jack, his brother. Jack Carlisle's the Big Squeeze in this county – '

'I hope you won't let his threats stop you.'

'Don't worry, they won't. This is one job that is going to be a great pleasure. I've never liked him anyway . . . and now will you please scram?'

'You wouldn't have me walk way down town alone at this hour of the night, would you?'

'All right, goddam it. I'll get Ulysses to take you home in my car – '

'But why do that? Why don't we do the simple thing?'

'I've told you before,' Dolan said, standing up. 'There are no extra beds.'

'That one looks good enough – '

'That's my bed.'

'I know it. Stop being stupid.'

'I'm not being stupid, for God's sake. I know what you want. I know I'm irresistible. I know I've got all the sex appeal in the world – '

'Swell. Now you're being you,' Myra said, smiling. 'Swell.'

' – but you're not going to sleep in my bed! Goddam it, I wish you'd stopped to get that cup of coffee that day!'

'Marvellous. I like to see you get steamed up. You're marvellous then.'

'You should see me throw women out of here at four o'clock in the morning. That's when I'm really marvellous. Now will – '

Somebody knocked at the door.

'Come in,' Dolan said, thinking it was one of the boys from downstairs, maybe Ulysses.

The door opened and in came April Coughlin Menefee.

'I didn't know you had company,' she said, looking un- perturbed at Myra. 'Am I intruding?'

'Why – no,' Dolan said, still surprised.

'That's nice,' April said, closing the door behind her.

Myra stood up, sucking in her breath audibly.

'Don't go,' April said, smiling, putting out her hand. 'My name is April Menefee. I've seen you around – '

'Hello!' Myra said, shaking hands.

' – Miss Barnovsky,' Dolan said, recovering from the first shock. 'My secretary. At the magazine, I mean. She helps me with the writing. Miss Barnovsky.'

'Yes, I know,' April said. 'Miss Barnovsky.'

'She's my secretary,' Dolan said, grinning foolishly.

'That's nice. I think you're awfully attractive,' April said to Myra.

'Thank you – '

'I'm so sorry you're going. Really. I'd like to know you better.'

'Good night, Mrs Menefee,' Myra said, starting out.

'Wait a minute,' Dolan said, following her to the door. 'I'll get Ulysses to drive you down – '

'Don't bother,' Myra said over her shoulder, walking through the darkness of the living-room, towards the stairs to the street . . .

'She's gorgeous, Mike. She looks like a girl in a Benda drawing. Now I see why you've been neglecting – '

'Oh, for God's sake, don't you ever have anything in your mind but sex?' Dolan said, closing the door.

'I'm pathological,' April said.

'You're insane. How'd you get in here?'

'Don't scowl so! I came in the back way, through Ulysses' room, and then up the inside staircase. Why?'

'Well, by God, this beats me,' Dolan said, shaking his head. 'You're the screwiest dame I ever saw. You've just been married, this is your wedding night, and you ask me why.'

'I ask you again: Why? What's wrong with coming here? "It is altogether fitting and proper – " or don't you remember Lincoln?'

'I give up,' Dolan said, sitting down on the studio bed, running his fingers through his hair. 'I positively give up. Everybody in town knows your car. Have you thought about what they'll be saying when they see it outside? They all know I live here.'

'I came in a taxi,' April said, taking off her coat.

'But what about Menefee?'

'Nothing about him. We had an argument and I got out of the car.'

'A swell way to start married life, that is.'

'The argument,' April said, coming over and sitting beside him on the bed, 'was about you. It started when he cut in on you at the dance, and it's been going ever since. Roy's very jealous of you.'

'Why the hell should he be jealous of me?'

'Maybe,' she said softly, looking at him with wide, innocent eyes, 'it's because you were a much more satisfactory lover than he was.'

'Well, I'll be goddamed,' Dolan said, staring at her in amazement. 'You told him that?'

'Certainly.'

'Oh, God,' Dolan groaned.

'That's not the only reason I came. I mean – not for that

alone. I've brought you something,' she said, opening her purse.
'I thought perhaps the finance company had been after you – I
know your car payment is due,' she said, laying a cheque beside
him.

The door burst open and Myra plunged in.

'There's a car just stopped in front and a man's getting out,'
she said, excited. 'I think it's your husband. A Packard coupé.'

'That's who it is, all right,' Dolan said, standing up. 'Get out
of here, April – down the back stairs.'

'Let him come,' April said doggedly. 'We may as well have
the showdown now as later.'

'Jesuschristyou'vegottogetout!'

'I'm not going,' April said calmly, relaxing, lying back on
the bed.

'Hurry!' Myra said.

Dolan rushed over and grabbed April by the arm, jerking her
to her feet. He turned her loose, stepped back, and taking deliberate aim, he slammed her in the jaw as hard as he could.
April uttered a little animal squeal and fell back unconscious
on the bed. Dolan leaned over, shovelling her into his arms.

'Throwthatcoataroundher – '

'Hurry!' Myra said, taking the coat, laying it over April's
body.

Swiftly Dolan went out the door, turning towards the back
stairs. There was no light back here in the long living-room,
but there was enough illumination from the street lamp outside
to show him the way. He turned out of the living-room to the
back hallway and hurried down to Ulysses' door, kicking
against it with his toes . . .

'What's the matter, Mister Mike?' Ulysses asked, opening
the door.

'Plenty,' Mike said, putting April's body on the cot. 'I'm in
a hell of a jam and all because of you, you black son of a bitch.
I told you before not to let April in the back way.'

'What's the matter with her, Mister Mike – '

'I socked her. Her husband's upstairs – '

'I wouldn't have let her in if I'd knowed she was married – '

'You'd do anything for five bucks, you bastard. Listen. I've got to go upstairs and pretend like I'm surprised to see the guy. Cover her over and see that she keeps quiet until he leaves. If she comes to and tries to get funny, slug her again. I'll come back when he leaves.'

'Okay, Mister Mike,' Ulysses said, throwing a quilt over April's body, completely covering it. 'Mister Mike – I didn't mean to get you in no jam – '

'It's all right. I guess I'm as much to blame as you are,' Dolan said, going out.

Outside his own door Dolan paused to light a cigarette, and then went inside. Myra was in the bed with a sheet held tightly under her chin and only her head visible. Roy Menefee was standing by the typewriter desk, his handsome face sullen.

'Well – hello!' Dolan said, pretending great surprise, looking from Myra to Roy and back again inquisitively. 'I never expected to see you here. Where's April?'

'That's what I'm trying to find out,' Menefee said.

'He thought she was here,' Myra said.

'Here? What would she be doing here? This is not a joke, is it? What happened, Roy?'

'April and I had an argument on the way home, and she said she'd rather walk than ride with me. I thought she was bluffing, so I stopped and let her out. I thought I'd teach her a lesson, so I drove around the block thinking I'd pick her up again – and when I got back she wasn't there.'

'You don't know April very well. She's not the bluffing kind.'

'I see that now. Naturally, I came here – '

'What made you think she'd be here?'

'Well – I don't know. She's always talking about you – '

'But why didn't you telephone first?'

'You wanted to catch her *flagrante delicto*, didn't you?' Myra said. 'That's Latin for in the act,' she explained to Dolan.

'I'm almost sorry to disappoint you, Roy – but she isn't here.'

'I see she isn't,' Menefee said. 'It's useless for me to tell you I'm sorry this happened, Dolan – '

'Forget it. She probably took a cab and went home. Why don't you try there?'

'I guess I will. Well . . . sorry to break in on you like this,' Menefee said, moving slowly towards the door. 'Could I speak to you a minute, Dolan?'

'Sure.'

They went outside to the living-room, and Dolan switched on the floor lamp by his door.

'I just wanted to ask you not to say anything about this – in the magazine – '

'All right, Roy, I promise. And I wish you'd try to get it through your brain that there's nothing between April and me now. I used to be nuts about her – but not any more. Her old man fixed that.'

'I believe you – '

'And I wish you wouldn't listen to Harry Carlisle. He'd like to have you believe a lot of things that aren't true.'

'I won't any more. Good night, Dolan,' Menefee said, taking Dolan's hand and shaking it. 'I'm sorry I disturbed you – '

'Forget it,' Dolan said, walking with him to the door to the stairs that led to the street. 'Good night.'

'Good night,' Menefee said, going down.

Dolan watched him through the window until he got in his car and drove off, and then he went down to Ulysses' room.

'. . . She's still out,' Ulysses said. 'You musta hit her with a baseball bat.'

'Get some water and let's get her out of here. Get a bucketful of water – '

Dolan yanked the quilt off her and started rubbing her wrists. There was still no flicker of consciousness. April lay like a corpse, and in the dim yellow light of Ulysses' small night lamp she looked like a corpse.

'Here you are, Mister Mike,' Ulysses said, coming back with the bucket of water. 'Did you get rid of him all right?'

'Yes – he even apologized for coming. Get her feet. We'll lay her on the floor – '

They laid her on the floor, and Dolan picked up the bucket of water and slammed it in April's face. She quivered under the impact of the cold water. Dolan raised her up to a sitting position and started shaking her. In a moment her lips moved and she grimaced, as you do when you taste a not-quite-ripe persimmon, and then she blinked her eyes and opened them.

'April! April!' Dolan said in her ear.

April smiled, looking around the room.

'Don't be alarmed; I'm all right now. Dolan, you son of a bitch,' she said, still smiling, 'you clipped me when I wasn't looking – '

'What a girl!' Dolan said, looking at Ulysses and grinning in spite of himself. 'Come on April, you've got to get out of here. Roy's just left – Ulysses, get on your shoes and coat and take Miss April through the back lot and put her in a cab.'

'Yes, sir,' Ulysses said, delighted to be a principal in one of Mr Mike's intrigues.

'I'm not going out any back way,' April said. 'I'm going out the way I came in.'

'You're going out the back way. I don't trust Menefee any too far. I think he believed the lie I told him, but he's jealous, and a guy who's jealous as hell is pretty cagey. He may be parked up the street right now waiting for you to come out.'

'Besides,' April said, 'I'm cold. Look what you've done to my hair.'

'Look what you've done to my life,' Dolan said. 'Come on – ' He helped her up.

'Go with Ulysses. You can always get a cab down at the corner. Got any money?'

'I've always got money, Mister Dolan – '

'I didn't know. I thought maybe you'd used all you had to bribe Ulysses. Go on, now – '

'I'm going – but I'll be back – '

'You do and I'll cut your throat. Ready, Ulysses?'

'Yes, sir.'

'Beat it then – '

Ulysses and April went out the back door. Dolan closed it behind them and went upstairs. He turned out the floor lamp and then went to the window that looked on the street below, peering out. There was no sign of a car. He smiled and went into his room.

'Well,' he said, looking at Myra's clothes neatly folded on the back of the chair, her shoes under the desk, 'and how have you been?'

'Is she gone?' Myra asked, turning on her side, raising on her elbow.

'Yes. I wish you'd go too.'

'Not a chance. Oh, by the way, here is a little souvenir your mad friend left,' she said, handing him the cheque April had written.

'Thanks,' Dolan said dryly, putting it in the pocket of his bathrobe.

'Haven't you any qualms about taking money from women?' Myra asked, amused at his nonchalance.

'Not when it's for value received,' Dolan said brutally.

'I see . . . Tell me, are all your nights as hectic as this one's been?'

'Hectic?' Dolan said, smiling coldly, taking off his robe, sitting on the edge of the bed. 'This one hasn't been hectic. This one has been very dull – '

'You're a wizard,' Myra said, putting her head back on the pillow. 'You're the damndest combination of charm and personality and heel that I've ever met . . .'

'Nuts,' Dolan said, snapping off the light . . .

*

A few days later Lawrence called him into the front office.

'This situation's pretty serious,' he said. 'You tell him, Eckman.'

'Well,' Eckman said, 'it all boils down to this: we're not getting any business for the *Cosmopolite*. The fifth number went on sale the other day, and how much business do you think we had in it?'

'I don't know,' Dolan said. 'Seven or eight pages, I think – '

'Five and a quarter,' Eckman said. 'Two of those were paid for. Two hundred dollars' worth.'

'And every issue costs us better than a thousand dollars,' Lawrence said. 'You can see where that leaves us.'

'Look,' Dolan said. 'I don't know much about the business end of this thing, but I'm damned if I see why we ought to give away three and four full-page ads a week. We ought to get something for those.'

'They're complimentaries. We have to give them away,' Eckman said. 'Those half-pages we gave the *Courier* and the *Times-Gazette* were in return for ten- and twelve-inch ads in their papers. The two-and-a-quarter other pages were to big stores to show them what we could do in the way of bringing them new trade – '

'Haven't we brought them new trade?'

'They say not,' Eckman said. 'You can see how difficult that makes it for me to actually sell them space.'

'Well, in the last four weeks Myra has got something like four hundred yearly subscriptions. That's two thousand dollars. Is that gone too?'

'Yes,' Lawrence said. 'You want to see the books?'

'No, I believe you. Only this comes as a sort of surprise to me. I thought we were doing fine – '

'We are doing fine,' Eckman said, 'as far as the editorial end is concerned. It's really a swell job of putting out a magazine. Just enough of everything. Except, of course, society. We've gone overboard on society.'

'That was no accident,' Dolan said. 'Put their names and pictures in the paper – that's the way to handle 'em. I know 'em.'

'We don't want to argue with you about that,' Lawrence said. 'That's a minor point. I'm satisfied with the magazine – and the publicity the baseball exposé got us. That put us in the public eye. But what good is all this unless we have sufficient business to pay the overhead?'

'Well, I don't know what to tell you,' Dolan said, shaking his head. 'All I can do is put out the best magazine I can – '

'Looks like there won't be any more,' Lawrence said.

'What? No more?'

'Not at a thousand dollars a week – a little better than a thousand dollars – '

'But won't you gamble a few weeks on it, Mr Lawrence? This can't miss! It's bound to hit! Hell, don't let me down now. Next week we're breaking the biggest story of the year. Bishop's working on it now.'

'I'm sorry, Dolan, I can't gamble – '

'An' I suppose it's no use to sell you on the idea that the story we're breaking next week ought to be printed?'

'It won't be worth a thousand dollars to me to have it printed,' Lawrence said. 'No story's worth that much to me, personally.'

'Well, it's worth it to me. Suppose I get the money to put out the next few issues – you know, like I did the first one?'

'We'd do it. Just so the expense is paid.'

'But would you keep on trying to sell ads for me, Eckman? This magazine might develop into a gold mine for you some day – '

'Certainly, I'll keep on. I'll work harder than ever for you – if that's possible. I'd like nothing better than to bring in all the business in town for you. I'm for you. I admire your spirit. I really believe you're idealistic about this thing – '

'Thanks. I'll try to have the money this afternoon – but don't stop plugging because I'll have it either today or tomorrow,' he said, going out, proceeding up the stairs to his own office.

Myra had the telephone in one hand, checking the long list of prospective subscribers with the other. Bishop was banging away at the typewriter.

'Where's Lillian?' Dolan asked.

'Out to the Country Club covering the women's golf tournament,' Myra said. 'Did you see Lawrence? He was asking for you – '

'Yes. Why the hell couldn't Lillian have covered the tournament by telephone? Or waited for the newspapers – '

'Not Lillian,' Myra said. 'She went out with her pencils and her little tablet – she couldn't brag about being society editor of the *Cosmopolite* if she had stayed in the office – '

'How's it going, Eddie?' Dolan asked, pausing beside him.

'Okay,' Bishop said, 'but for God's sake stop peeking over my shoulder. You know how that unnerves me. You're worse than Thomas.'

'Sorry. I called you a couple of times last night – '

'I was out. You got any idea where this McAlister woman lives? To hell and gone out by the county orphanage. Almost to Cold Springs.'

'Did you see her?'

'Yeah, had a long talk with her. She says her daughter died of acute indigestion. Mrs Griffith said the same thing. Begins to look like that was all old Doc Estill knew how to write.'

'They didn't suspect what you were after – '

'No, I brought it all out casually. I found out another thing in our favour, too. Neither one of the mothers had ever heard of Estill. He was suggested when Elsie Griffith was very ill with the poison. Of course, Mrs McAlister never heard of him until the certificate was signed. But then she wouldn't. Fay McAlister died on the operating-table. This goddam Carlisle's a mass murderer – '

'I wish we could locate the guys that knocked 'em up – '

'We can locate 'em. But you can't prove it. You can't prove

any part of this business. Even the girls who went to Carlisle and got away with it won't talk. You can cause an investigation, but what the hell? Carlisle'll be whitewashed. You can exhume the McAlister and Griffith girls, but that won't do any good. By now they're nothing but bones – '

'Just write the story, Ed. I'll handle the details.'

'All right. I hope to hell you know what you're doing. When the Grand Jury calls you, you'd better have something to tell 'em.'

'I'll have it. Myra – get Mrs Marsden on the phone for me, will you?'

'What's her number?' Myra asked, narrowing her eyes, biting her lips.

'Look it up in the book, will you?' Dolan said, staring thoughtfully at the wall . . .

'That will be all, Emery,' Mrs Marsden said, as the butler placed the tray on the Renaissance coffee-table. 'How do you like your tea, Michael – straight or cream and sugar or lemon?'

'Cream and sugar and lemon,' Dolan said.

'All three?'

'Er – yes, please,' Dolan said, realizing from her tone that he had said the wrong thing. 'Isn't that right to ask for all three? I never had tea before. I don't know.'

'You're the most refreshing person I've ever met,' Mrs Marsden said, smiling. 'You're so naïve. Suppose you try it with just cream and sugar.'

'All right – '

'Two lumps?'

'Yes, thank you,' he said, taking the tea. 'I didn't mean to put you to any trouble – '

'Oh, no trouble . . .'

'Heard from Mary Margaret lately? . . .'

'Yesterday. She loves Mexico City.'

'I don't blame her. I like foreign cities too. Some day I'm

going to Mexico City – and the South Seas.'

'Have you ever been to the South Seas?'

'Only sitting in the last row of a movie theatre. That's not very satisfactory.'

'I thought I'd take a trip in the fall. A cruise to the islands – '

'That'll be swell. I'll bet Mary Margaret'll like that. She loves to travel.'

'I wouldn't take her,' Mrs Marsden said. 'That wouldn't be much fun for me. Wouldn't you like to go?'

'Me? Oh, I couldn't – '

'Why not? You could be in Los Angeles and I could happen through and – '

'It'd be marvellous, but – '

'Why not? More tea?'

'No, thanks. Oh, I just couldn't. I've got the magazine – '

'You think you'll have it by then?'

'I hope so – the way it looks now I won't, though. That's why I came out to see you. I don't know who else to go to. I was wondering – '

'Money? – '

'Yes. Temporary, of course. It's not well established yet, but as soon as it is, the business houses will give us ads and then we'll be all right. We can pay back the people who've had confidence in us – '

'How much money will it take to ferry you over?'

'Well, it takes about a thousand a week – '

'And how many weeks before you will be able to make expenses?'

'Oh, a couple of weeks. Maybe three.'

'Mightn't it take six?'

'It might – '

'Then you want to borrow six thousand dollars?'

'Yes, but, of course, I'll pay you back – '

'Yes, yes, I know,' Mrs Marsden said, smiling wisely, standing up. 'I'll write you a cheque, Michael. But why don't you take this money and go away somewhere – and have a good time and forget the magazine? There'd be some point to giving it to you then – '

'The magazine means too much to me – the town needs it. You know what I'm trying to do with it – '

'That's why I don't see why you don't take the money and go away. To Los Angeles, say – until fall . . .'

'I can't – '

'Well – if you haven't had your illusions shattered by now, I won't do it. But you know you've picked out a sort of herculean job, don't you?'

'Sure – '

' – My cheque-book's upstairs in my bedroom. You'd better come along and tell me who to make it out to,' Mrs Marsden said, moving away . . .

Six-feet one, a hundred and ninety-five pounds of forty-four-year-old he-man, with a brown walrus moustache, Bud McGonagill looked exactly what he was supposed to look like, a peace officer. He was the sheriff of Colton county.

'I thought I'd best come here,' he said, looking around Dolan's room. 'Nice place you got – '

'Yeah, comfortable. What's the beef, Bud?'

'No beef, Mike. I didn't want to do any talking in my office. Best not to take chances. That's why I waited till dark to come.'

'You're right. Well, sit down, Bud, there's no dictaphones in here. How've you been?'

'Okay. Ain't seen you in a month – '

'I've been pretty busy with the magazine – '

'Good magazine, Mike. I like it. I guess it's a relief from working on the paper – '

'It certainly is. Imagine what a relief it'd be to you if you could go out and pinch people who ought to be pinched. It's the same thing.'

'That day won't never come for me, Mike. There'll always

be them that's hooked up right with the Big Boys. It gripes me, but I can't do nothing about it like you. Hell, I got three kids in college – '

'How're they doing? How's Terry?'

'Fine, just fine. Terry wrote me he'd heard from you – '

'I wrote him before I left the paper. Swell kid. Great football player. All-American next season, Bud – '

'I dunno, since you're off the paper. You done a lot for Terry – getting publicity in the big papers and magazines – '

'Terry doesn't need me, Bud. He's a cinch all-American. He'd made it last year but for the advance advertising Wilson and Grayson and Berwanger got. You know how that is. You need a year's build-up before you're selected – '

'I hope so. Mind if I smoke?'

'Certainly not. Come on, Bud, spill it. You're a lousy actor.'

'Well – I been hearing things about you, Mike,' McGonagill said slowly.

'What kind of things?'

'Some of the boys been hearing a lot of talk around the courthouse about you and your magazine. Seems like you're going to clean up the county or something.'

'Sooner or later I'll get around to it, but that oughtn't to bother you, Bud. You're on the level.'

'Oh, I ain't afraid of no investigation or anything like that. I been a pretty good sheriff, I guess. I ain't worried about me. I'm worried about you.'

'Me?'

'Yeah. That's what I wanted to talk to you about. I didn't know whether you realized what you were up against.'

'I ought to. That's all I've heard since I started the magazine – what I was up against and what was liable to happen to me. But that isn't going to stop me, Bud. I'm a hard-headed Mick. I've got my neck bowed. I've got enough money to keep the thing going now whether anybody advertises or not, and I've got my neck bowed.'

'Mike, I like you. You've done a lot for me – and for Terry, getting that scholarship and everything – but you're trying to make a pair of deuces beat three aces. Now, I been around this county a hell of a long time – and I know what's what.'

Dolan came around and stood before him.

'You're swell to come here, Bud – and I appreciate it. But I'm going through with this. I'm sick of all this goddam thieving and conniving and murdering. I could never spend another peaceful night if I quit now.'

'By God, I'm glad you said that,' McGonagill said, sticking out his hand. 'I'm for you. I told Jack Carlisle you wouldn't – '

'Did Jack Carlisle send you here?'

'He asked me to drop by. He knew we were friends. He wanted me to sort of tell you he wouldn't want to be annoyed by no bad publicity – '

'So that's why you came?'

'Nope, I could have said that over the phone. I came to bring you this – ' he reached into his pocket, taking out a paper and a badge. 'This is a special deputy's commission – and here's your badge. I kind of thought maybe you might feel a little better if you had 'em.'

'Well – thanks, Bud,' Dolan said, a lump in his throat.

'Oh, that ain't all. Here,' he said, taking a pistol and holster out of his hip pocket. 'They ain't much good without this. That's a .380 automatic – already got four notches on it. Belonged to Percy Yard. You remember Percy – '

'Sure, I remember. Hell, Bud – this is damned swell of you.'

'I dated the commission back six months so's nothing could be said. That's a swell gun, Mike. I hope you don't have to use it, but if you do it'll be nice to know it's on the side of right instead of the side it was on.'

'Well, I don't know what to say, Bud. I hope I don't have to use it. If I got in a jam I'd probably get so excited I'd shoot myself with it. I don't think I'll need it – '

'You'd better have it, anyway. You got a right to carry it. I guess if Jack Carlisle can get special commissions for his own thugs, I can get one for a pal of mine. What's this story you're going to print about his brother? About his abortions?'

'You know anything about him?' Dolan asked, surprised.

'A little. I know a girl used to work for him – '

'What was her name?'

'I don't remember just now. I can find out.'

'Will you, Bud? Will you find out? Maybe she could help me – '

'Sure. I'll telephone you. Where can I get you?'

'Lawrence Publishing Company. Maybe I'd better phone you?'

'I can remember that all right – well, Mike, anything I can do – you know, anything on the q.t. – just sound off. You know the kind of spot I'm in and everything – '

'I know. I'll be careful, Bud. Thanks again for everything,' Dolan said, shaking hands, walking out with him.

'Keep your head up, Mike,' McGonagill said . . .

Dolan finished reading Bishop's story and looked at Myra.

'What do you think?'

'Swell,' Myra said. 'You're swell too. First time I've seen you in a tuxedo. Where're you going?'

'I'm talking about the story,' Dolan said.

'It's got all the facts,' Bishop said. 'I still don't think we can nail Carlisle with this alone, but at least we can start the ball rolling.'

'I told you not to worry about the details – '

'I just don't want the Grand Jury to catch us with our pants down, that's all.'

'They won't – '

'Who're we going after next?'

'Your old pal, Nestor. We're going to find out how a police commissioner can build a big home in Weston Park and ride in a Deusenberg on four thousand a year – '

'That'll be fun,' Bishop said. 'I'll enjoy that. Of course,' he went on airily, 'the most fun'll come when they strap me in the electric chair or blow the top of my head off.'

'It won't be that bad,' Dolan said, struggling with his tie. 'All those guys are yellow.'

'Yeah? Well, I hope you're right – '

'My, my,' Myra said. 'Aren't you beginning to look elegant? Would you like to have some help with your tie?'

'Thanks, I can manage. And I don't like your cheap goddam sarcasm either.'

'Now, was I being sarcastic?' Myra said, turning to Bishop. 'Was I? I merely remarked that you looked elegant and you bark at me. What's the matter – guilty conscience?'

'Why should I have a guilty conscience?'

'Oh – many reasons. You might be going out with Lillian or – '

'Lillian? What gave you that idea?'

'Well, you see, I'm a logician,' Myra explained. 'She is a beautiful girl, and she is very high in society and her father also has loads of money, and she has a very bad case of what is vulgarly known as hot pants for you. All those qualities in a girl have attracted you in the past, so I naturally presumed they would continue to attract you.'

'Look. I'm putting on this tuck because I haven't worn it in a couple of months,' Dolan said patiently, spreading his hands. 'I am positively going no place in particular. I am going to drop in at the Little Theatre soon, just casually, as if I had already been some place where I had to dress. I want to take a quick look at the new show which opened night before last and say "hello" to David, to whom I still owe fifteen hundred bucks – and say "hello" to the very few people who are still my friends. Does that satisfy your goddam curiosity?'

'Not bad, not bad,' Myra said. 'You certainly make it sound convincing. It's too bad you had to give up acting.'

'For God's sake, Ed – will you get this dame out of here before I cut her throat?'

'I'd love to oblige you, but I've got to get home. One of the kids is down with the flu. Anything else you wanted to see me about?'

'No; the Carlisle story was all. Thanks for bringing it over.'

'Okay. Good night,' Bishop said, getting up, going out.

'Why don't you go home, too?' Dolan said to Myra, slipping into his coat.

'I don't feel like going back to that hall bedroom. I feel like staying here. I'll make myself comfortable – '

'I get it. You think I'm going to bring a girl home with me, don't you?'

'Now, what on earth ever gave you that idea?' Myra said. 'I trust you implicitly, Michael – implicitly. I trust you just as far as I can throw that bookcase with both hands tied behind me.'

'Oh, God,' Dolan said.

'And if I were you,' Myra went on, 'I wouldn't bring any young woman home with me. It would be a little uncomfortable sleeping three in that bed.... Aren't you forgetting something?' she asked, stopping him at the door. 'Don't you want your new automatic?'

'You keep it. Do me a favour and stick the front end in your mouth and pull the trigger. But not on my bed. Those are fresh sheets . . .'

When Dolan got backstage the show was almost over, the fourth act of *Anna Christie*, the scene where Burke tells Anna he has signed on the *Londonderry* for Cape Town. Dolan stood in the wings for a few minutes, looking, wondering who the new man was playing Burke, then he walked on back through the big fire-door and downstairs to the Bamboo Room. Johnny London, David, and April were lounging on the wicker furniture.

'Hello, April – '

'Hello, Mike,' she said, standing up.

'Well – I see your hair finally dried – '

'I think I'll live over it,' she said, abruptly going out.

'What's the matter with her?' Dolan asked, puzzled.

'Maybe it's the shock of seeing you around the theatre,' David said. 'What are you made up for?'

'I just came from a party. How're you, Johnny?'

'Fine. You're looking prosperous – '

'Two more payments and it's mine. Who's the fellow playing Burke? I thought Pat Mitchell was doing it – '

'Pat's got the mumps. This chap's name's Wycoff,' David said. 'Learned the part in eight hours. How'd you like him?'

'I only saw a few minutes of him. Looked good – '

'He ought to. He's been in stock for years.'

'What's April doing around here? She in the show?'

'No – you tell him, Johnny – '

'None of my business. You tell him.'

'April's got a crush on Emil,' David said, grinning.

'You mean Emil, the electrician?'

'That's the one – '

'When did this start?'

'Three or four days ago. Only this time she's really blown her topper. Says she can't live without him. She was telling us about his poetic soul when you came in – '

'So that's why she left. What does Roy Menefee say about it, Johnny?'

'He's sore as hell, but what can he do? Poor bastard, I feel sorry for him. If she were my wife, I'd punch her in the nose.'

'She needs it, all right,' Dolan said. 'Where's the Major?'

'On stage somewhere, I guess – '

'I think I'll stroll up. See you one of these days, Dave, and have a long talk and make a report – '

'No hurry, Mike – '

'So long,' Dolan said, walking out.

On the steps he met Timothy Adamson.

'Could I speak to you a minute, Mike?' he asked.

'Sure, Tim – come on upstairs – '

'I'm glad you came here,' Timothy said, following him up to the corridor. 'I was going to see you tomorrow – '

'What's on your mind?'

'You know how long I've been around this theatre, don't you, Mike?'

'Yes. Couple of years – '

'Nearer three. And in those three years I've never had a good part. I'm always the understudy. I'm not squawking about that, because there was no chance to use me until a month ago. Remember when you walked out of *Lilion*? They gave it to David. Now Pat Mitchell gets the mumps and they put some new guy, some old-time stock actor, in the part of Burke. It's goddam unfair.'

'I think it is too, Tim, but why don't you speak to the Major about it?'

'I did. He says he can't trust me in a big part, because I haven't had the experience. How the hell am I going to get the experience if he won't trust me? God, I'd rather act than eat. I want to get somewhere in the theatre. There was no reason for putting that new guy in the part of Burke. I know that part perfectly. How can I ever be a good actor if I don't ever get started?'

'You're right, Tim – dead right. What do you want me to do?'

'You could speak to the Major – '

'That wouldn't do any good. He's off me.'

'Well, I see your magazine, and I think what you're trying to do is swell. Can't you write something about this situation around here? Hell, they break a guy's heart. I wouldn't be asking you to do it, but after all this is supposed to be a Little Theatre – where people with talent have a chance. It's supposed to be wide open. The way it is it's worse than a Broadway show.'

'You're perfectly right – perfectly.'

'Will you write something in your magazine? You're the only
guy in town who can straighten this thing out – '

'Yes – I'll write something. I definitely will.'

'Don't be sore at me for asking you – '

'Sore at you? Listen. This is the nicest thing anybody
has ever done for me. This is the nicest compliment I ever
got.'

'Thanks, Mike.'

'Thank you, Tim. Have you seen the Major?'

'He's over on that side – by the switchboard – '

Dolan nodded and walked through the corridor, past the
dressing-rooms, and through the other fire-door on to the stage
right. There were several people standing around, and when his
eyes had adjusted themselves to the darkness he made out April
and Emil, the electrician, in a corner by the switchboard, standing close together.

'She's an indiscreet little bitch,' Dolan said to himself, looking around for the Major. Finally he saw him and went over and
tapped him on the shoulder, motioning for him to come back
into the corridor. In a moment they tiptoed off.

'Have to sort of keep an eye on him,' the Major said. 'First
night, you know.'

'You prompting?'

'No, just standing by. Well, Dolan, how are you?'

'All right – '

'You look fine in that outfit – only you know what you
should be doing, don't you?'

'What?'

'Out there playing Burke. Made to order for you – '

'That guy seems to be doing all right. Who is he?'

'Name's Wycoff. Learned the part in eight hours.'

'I mean – where'd he come from? I don't recall seeing him
around – '

'I dug him up . . . Congratulations on your magazine. Hear
a lot of talk about it.'

'You'll hear a lot more, I hope . . . I understand Pat Mitchell got the mumps on you – '

'Yes; too bad.'

'Major, why didn't you give that part to Timothy?'

'Oh, now, come, Dolan. After all, I have to do what I think best. I've got the box-office to consider. Has Timothy been talking to you?'

'I haven't seen him in a month. I knew he'd been hanging around here for three years waiting for a chance, and when I saw this new man on stage I wondered, that's all – '

'Timothy'll get his chance. But let's talk about you.'

'I don't want to talk about me. I want to find out what you're going to do about turning this joint back into a Little Theatre – where people can have a chance to develop themselves – '

'And I don't want to talk about that,' the Major said curtly. 'This theatre is my responsibility, and I'm going to direct it the way I think is best.'

'But you forget this is a community affair, and that the people who support it have something to say – '

'Are you going to write this up in your magazine?' the Major asked suddenly.

'I might – '

'Then I've nothing to say.'

'All right, but I'm giving you a chance. Do you want to have David write me a statement I can use? I'd like to have your side of it.'

'I want nothing to do with it. You come here belligerently, looking for trouble – '

'I did no such goddam thing. I came here to say "hello" to a few friends I hadn't seen in a long time. I saw the new man in the part, and that's why I wondered why Timothy wasn't given a chance – '

'You can't scare me – '

'I'm not trying to,' Dolan said.

The fire-door opened and through it rolled the sound of the applause from the auditorium.

'Excuse me,' the Major said, going on stage . . .

Dolan walked out the stage door to the patio, through the patio to the alley behind the theatre where he had parked his car. He got in behind the wheel, lighted a cigarette, and settled down to wait.

'Where do you want to go?' Dolan asked, as they rolled along through Sycamore Park.

'The Hot Spot,' Lillian said. 'I'm hungry.'

'I don't want to go there – '

'Why not?'

'Simply because for the first time in my life I'm using a little judgement. You're the only girl in town whose name hasn't been connected with mine, and I'm not going to the Hot Spot and let your friends see us together. If it got back to your family it might be awkward for you.'

'I'm not worried about my family. I'm twenty years old – '

'Just the same, we're not going – '

'Are you afraid of Myra?'

'Myra? Certainly not. She's nothing to me – '

'She thinks she is. She as much as told me to let you alone – '

'When did she say that?'

'From time to time. That's why I made the date with you – just to spite her.'

'You've got a lot of guts,' Dolan said, sore.

'Oh, I didn't mean that literally,' she said, moving over a little closer. 'You know how I've always felt about you, Mike – '

'All right,' he said, still surly. 'I'll see that you get fed.'

Nothing was said for a few blocks.

'What exactly did Myra say to you about me?' he asked finally.

'I don't remember – exactly. But it was to the effect that I'd better let you alone.'

'Is that as close as you can come?'

'Oh – she said something about you being a child in some things and susceptible to girls, because they were wealthy and social – I don't know – a lot of junk I didn't pay any attention to – '

'She did, hunh?' Dolan said grimly.

Nothing was said for a couple more blocks.

'Lillian – how'd you like to get married?' Dolan asked.

'I'd like it,' Lillian said.

'I mean how'd you like to marry me?'

'That's what I mean,' she said calmly.

'All right – can you postpone the sandwich till after the wedding?'

'You can't get married at this time of night – '

'Can't I? I'll get the licence-clerk out of bed and then get Judge Palmer. He's a Justice of the Peace. He'll marry us – '

'But, Mike,' Lillian said, beginning to get a little excited now. 'What about the ring?'

'We'll borrow one. He's the marrying Judge. He ought to have a prop ring somewhere. But what about the money? Got any money?'

'A little. About fifteen dollars – '

'That's enough. Here we go,' he said, turning around in the middle of the block, going back to the drug-store to telephone . . .

At two o'clock that morning Mr and Mrs Michael Dolan sat at the counter of a small all-night café on lower Front Street near the courthouse. They had finished eating, and now they were waiting for the rain to finish raining.

'. . . Well,' Lillian said, 'here we are – '

'Yes, here we are,' Dolan said, laughing. 'You know that story?'

'What story?'

'That one. "Well, here we are – " '

'Is it risqué?'

'It's not that kind of story at all. It's a short story. A magazine story by Dorothy Parker. About a couple that just got married – '

'Yes?'

'Never mind, forget it,' Dolan said, looking at the window, watching the raindrops slide down. 'You like the rain?'

'No – '

'I love it. I wish it would rain all the time. It reminds me of the war.'

'I shouldn't think you'd want to be reminded of the war after the way you got shot.'

'I don't mean the war, exactly – I mean France. It reminds me of France.'

'Paris?'

'Tours. Blois. Down in the château country – '

'Well, I wish it would hurry up and stop. Mike, where are we going?'

'You mean tonight?'

'Yes – '

'I don't know. I guess you better go home. We can talk this over in the morning – '

'What is there to talk over? We're married, aren't we?'

'Yes; but there are a lot of things to be done. First of all, I've got to get you a wedding-ring and return that one to the Judge. Then I suppose I'll have to have a talk with your father – sooner or later – '

'He's in San Francisco.'

'He is? That's swell! That gives me a little time to figure things out. Look. Don't say anything about this, will you, Lillian? For a while? This marriage will meet with a lot of opposition, and we've got to have time to get ourselves set.'

'But, Mike – why can't we go somewhere tonight and talk?'

'We could talk right here. It's not that. It's time I want. I've got to think – '

'You didn't act like this two hours ago,' Lillian said, pouting a little.

'Oh, don't get me wrong. I'm not a second-guesser. I don't ever regret anything I do. But you must admit it was rather sudden – '

'I wish we could go to a hotel. I'm going to catch hell for this anyway – I might as well get some kind of dividend – '

'Come on, the rain's slackened up,' Dolan said, sliding off the stool. 'You're going home – '

After he had left her at the front door (without kissing her good night) he drove aimlessly around in the drizzling rain, fascinated, as always, by the shining streets and the wetness of the smell and the utter loneliness of the city:

buzz

buzz

buzz

buzz

buzz.

The wheels in his head went, his mind not thinking about any one thing in particular but trying to think of one thing in particular, as a man surfeited and satiated and nauseated by too much sex tries to concentrate when he is having an affair with a lovely girl, tries desperately and fails, thinking of everything else – but not that . . .

Finally he gave up and went home, climbing through a window downstairs and feeling his way through the dark into Ernst's room. He switched on the light. Ernst was sleeping like a log, snoring and gurgling and raising hell. Dolan went over and shook him out of it.

'What's the matter?' Ernst said in his thickly flavoured speech, blinking his eyes, quite peaceful now.

'Move over,' Dolan said, starting to undress.

'What's the matter with your bed?' Ernst asked quietly.

'It's being used. Myra.'

'Again?'

'Yes – '

'You're a fool, Mike. She's an attractive woman.'

'I know it – '

'Is that rain?' Ernst asked, raising up, just now conscious of
the dripdrip-dripdrip of the water from the roof.

'Yes – '

Ernst got out of bed, going to the window, looking out. He
wore no pyjamas. In a few seconds he turned back into the
room, a smile on his face.

'I love the rain,' he said. 'Reminds me of the old country – '

'Germany?'

'Yes,' he said, getting back into bed.

'Reminds me of France.'

'The war?'

'In a way – '

'Where were you nineteen years ago tonight?'

'In the St Mihiel. Where were you?'

'In the St Mihiel. On the side of Mont Sec.'

'That's funny. I was at Essey. Nineteen years ago tomorrow
I got that,' he said, pointing to the shrapnel scar on his right
thigh that looked like the map of Florida. 'Maybe your battery
gave me that – '

'Maybe – '

Dolan turned out the light and went back to the bed, groping
for the covers.

'Move over,' he said, sliding down under the sheet.

'You're lucky you didn't get killed – '

'Am I? . . .' Dolan said, turning over.

It was still raining when Dolan reached the office that morning.
Only Myra was there, reading the page proofs.

'Good morning,' she said, putting on a charming smile.

'It is, at that, isn't it?' Dolan said, putting his trench coat and hat on the hall tree. 'From horizon to horizon nothing but those beautiful grey clouds. Looks like they hold all the rain in the world – '

'Michael Dolan Shelley,' Myra said, smiling, not so charmingly. 'You're not one of those people who go walking in the rain?'

'I used to until Garbo got all that publicity. Then I stopped it. I didn't want to appear affected. How's it look?'

'This? – Oh, perfect. I had it set up, and I've checked it all over. Nothing to do but bind it – '

'Thanks,' Dolan said, sitting down at his desk. 'I overslept.'

'Was it fatigue – or Ernst?'

'How'd you know I slept with Ernst?'

'I was watching the rain too. I saw you drive up. You climbed in downstairs through the window.'

'I guess I ought to be sore at you – but I'm not.'

'You've got no reason to be. I purposely left early this morning so you could change clothes without the embarrassment of seeing me there. Mike – '

'What?' Dolan said, not looking at her, looking at the desk.

'I won't bother you any more. I won't come to your room again.'

'That's all right, Myra – '

'No, it isn't – it's all wrong. I've been an ass. But believe me,' she said, getting up, moving to his desk, looking down at him, 'I was only trying to help you.'

'Help me? Help me what, for God's sake?' he asked, compelled, finally, to look at her.

'Now, don't growl and don't be irritated. I hate those mechanisms of yours – '

'And I hate this smug attitude of yours – this goddam maternal business. Where the hell do you get off to give me advice?'

'Somebody ought to. It's the one thing you need. Mike,' she said, sitting on the desk, one foot on the floor, 'you'd be a great man – a great power – if you'd take advice. You're a born leader, but you're too impetuous, too impulsive, too obstinate – '

'Oh, for God's sake,' Dolan said, slamming the desk with his palms, standing up, glaring at her. 'I wonder why the hell I don't smack you right in the nose – '

'Maybe it's because you know I'm right,' Myra said, unintimidated.

Dolan bit his lip, turned abruptly, and strode to her desk. He snatched up the page proofs and went downstairs to the mechanical department and gave them to Cully, the foreman.

'Okay, Cully – let 'em go,' he said.

He walked back to the front door and stood looking out into the street, watching the street car come down the hill, staring at the front end with morbid fascination, wondering what it would be like to run out and throw himself under the wheels, wondering how painful it would be, wondering how long before the end would come . . .

'Prescott of the *Courier* just telephoned,' Myra said, when he got back into the office.

'All right. Hello, Ed. When did you get here?'

'A minute ago. I parked in the alley. I yelled at you as I came up – '

'Did you?' Dolan said, surprised.

'Yeah. You were standing in the front – '

'Yes. How are the kids?'

'Only one. Okay. Fever, you know – '

Dolan sat down and dialled the *Courier* and asked for Prescott. The girl in the city room told him to try the Press Room at the courthouse. Dolan broke the connexion and dialled the Press Room.

'Allan Prescott,' he said. '. . . Hello – this is Mike Dolan . . . Yes . . . Oh, wait a minute, Allan – you can't print that! . . . Yes . . . Well, not yet . . . I don't know – maybe next week, maybe next month, maybe I'll never use it. That's why, you see? . . . He did? How'd you find that out? – He did? . . . He

did? . . . Well, you tell the old sonofabitch I'll see that he gets
it back . . . Oh, sure, sure, suresuresure, print any goddam thing
you like . . .' Dolan said, as he hung up the telephone.

Myra and Bishop were both looking at him.

'What's the matter?' Bishop asked.

'Nothing – not a goddam thing.'

'What is it?' Bishop said. 'Hell, I couldn't help overhearing.
What'd Prescott want? What's he got you're trying to keep out
of the paper?'

'Nothing. Nothing.'

'All right, if you want to act like that – okay. I thought we
were all friends. My mistake.'

Dolan said nothing, sat looking at them, but not seeing them
clearly, not having his eyes focused on them.

'I'll tell you,' Myra said. 'This crazy bastard got married last
night.'

'He – what?'

'Married. Oh,' she said to Dolan, 'you needn't look so dazed!
Lillian phoned me this morning and told me all about it. She
couldn't wait to broadcast it. And with embellishment. I know
all about the ring you borrowed from the judge – and about
how you took her straight home – '

'Well, I'll be a sonofabitch!' Bishop said, sitting down. 'And
Lillian – of all people!'

'Why not?' Myra said. 'She's beautiful, and she's got social
position, and her father's president of one of the biggest banks
on the Pacific coast and an ex-Senator to boot. That's what this
crazy bastard wanted. It doesn't matter that she's a cheap little
bitch who's got a yellow streak up her back – '

Dolan shoved himself up from the desk, blood in his eyes,
and started around towards Myra, his fists clenched. Bishop
grabbed him and held him.

'Cool off – sit down, Mike – '

Dolan stood still in Bishop's arms, trembling in every muscle
of his body, looking at Myra, livid hatred on his face.

'It's the truth,' Myra said, continuing in the same biting tone. 'She's a yellow little bitch. She had hot pants for you, and she didn't have the guts to lay you and get it over with. She had to marry you! Well, you should have taken her last night because today she'll probably look for ways to crawl out of it. Her mother'll be after her and all her friends – and all the papers, all over the front pages – oh, Heavens, you poor crazy bastard – '

She stopped, turned, and walked rapidly out of the office to the rest-room.

'Sit down, Mike,' Bishop said, releasing him. 'Sit down – '

Dolan went back to the desk and sat down.

'I don't guess it's quite as hopeless as it sounds,' Bishop said, lighting a cigarette. 'There must be something we can do.'

'Myra's jealous – she's jealous as hell.'

'I wouldn't know about that – but she's also right. She's right as right can be. I don't see how you get sucked in by these broads, Mike – I swear to God I don't. That Lillian has been on the make for you since she's been here. I wouldn't be at all surprised if she didn't suggest this job herself – '

'It hasn't occurred to either one of you that I might be in love with her, has it?' Dolan said, calmer now.

'Nuts,' Bishop said. 'If you'll pardon my French – nuts! You know her people are going to be furious about this. Why, everybody west of the Rockies knows old lad Fried is hipped on the subject of ancestry. You remember that story they tell in every city room in town – that she won't even sit in a chair unless it's got a coat of arms painted on it. Hell, she lugged Lillian all over Europe last year trying to marry her off to a title. Won't you ever learn you're poison to the Weston Park fathers? What do you suppose her old man's going to say about this?'

'He's in San Francisco – '

'You mean he *was* in San Francisco. You can bet your right eye he's on the way home by now – '

Dolan had a sandwich and a glass of milk at a drug-store on the edge of Weston Park, and then went to the telephone, calling Lillian's house again. Neither Mrs Fried nor *Miss* Fried had returned, the butler said. Dolan asked when they were expected. Well, did he know where *Miss* Fried could be reached? No, the butler said, but the Senator was returning from the north by plane sometime in the afternoon, and undoubtedly *he* could be reached around seven o'clock. Dolan slammed up the receiver and went out and got in his car. He sat there a few minutes, burning, and then decided to go to the house himself.

He parked the car half a block away and then went down the street and up the long steps to the big veranda. A Negro man in a white coat answered the bell, holding the door half-open, cautiously.

'Miss Lillian here?' Dolan asked.

'No, sir,' the Negro said firmly.

Dolan put his foot against the bottom of the door, pushing and going inside to the ornate entrance hall. The Negro did not try to stop him.

'Lillian!' he called, up the stairs. 'Lillian!'

There was no answer.

'She isn't here, sir – '

'Where'd she go?'

'She didn't say. She went out early this morning with her mother – '

'Did you give her my messages?'

'I gave them to her mother. Mrs Fried's instructions – '

Dolan nodded and walked out, going back to his car.

'I'm glad it's still raining,' he said to himself . . .

He drove around a couple of hours and then went back to the apartment, putting his car in the garage and then going upstairs. Ulysses was in the living-room, wiping the window-sills where the rain had leaked through.

'Anybody call?'

'Yes, sir – Miss April and a Mr Thomas. He said it was important.'

'That all? None from Miss Lillian?'

'No, sir – '

Dolan went on into his room, taking off his trench coat and hat and throwing them on the desk. He lighted a cigarette and sat down on the edge of the bed. In a minute or two Ulysses came in.

'Seen the papers, Mister Mike?'

'About me?'

'Yes, sir. They said you got married – '

'I did, Ulysses. Early this morning.'

'Miss Lillian did come around here, did she, Mister Mike?'

'No, I don't think so. Blonde. Big girl. Pretty.'

'I'll say she is. Her picture's in the paper. She's very pretty. Are you gonna move, Mister Mike?'

'I don't know – sit down, Ulysses.'

Ulysses sat down, draping the wet rag over the metal waste-basket.

'The reason I asked you is because it looks like we're all gonna have to move, and maybe you getting married was a good thing. That man was around here this afternoon – '

'What man?'

'You know, the agent. Mrs Ratcliff's agent. He said if they put over a deal with the oil company they'll tear down the house and put up a big gas station here.'

'Well, I guess it's time we got thrown out. We can't go on for ever without paying rent – '

'But this old house is falling to pieces, Mister Mike. Nobody wants to rent this place.'

'That's why Mrs Ratcliff has put us on the cuff so long. It'll be tough on the other boys.'

'Sure will. There ain't two dollars between 'em. If you hadn't fed 'em, they'd of starved long ago.'

'Maybe they'd been better off, Ulysses. Have you been here all day?'

'Yes, sir – '

'And you're sure Miss Lillian didn't call?'

'Yes, sir. Nobody but them two I told you – Miss April and the man from the *Times-Gazette*.'

'Well. I've got myself into a mess, Ulysses – '

'Seems to me, Mister Mike, that you's always in a mess,' Ulysses said, grinning.

'This one's a honey.'

'Her people?'

'Yes. Her old man's liable to take a shot at me – '

'You tell me what he looks like, and I'll see he don't get in here.'

'I'm not as much worried about that as I am why I'm such a goddam fool when it comes to women. Why am I, Ulysses?'

'I don't know, sir. If I knew the answer to that I could save myself a lot of misery – '

' – Look, Ulysses. I'm going to try to get some sleep. If Miss Lillian calls, wake me up – '

'All right, sir,' Ulysses said, taking the rag off the waste-basket, standing up. 'Is there something I can do for you – fix a hot bath or something?'

'No, but tell you what you can do: If you see a grey-haired, distinguished gentleman at the door with a machine-gun, yell and start running . . .'

When Dolan woke up the first thing he was conscious of was that it was still raining and that there was something in his stomach, directly under his navel, that was warm and cheerful; and then he was aware that the lights were on and that some-body was in the room and that he was being shaken. When he opened his eyes he saw Bishop bending over him, and when Bishop saw his eyes open he sat down on the bed beside him.

'Mike – are you awake?'

'I'm awake. What's the matter?'

'It's about the magazine – '

'What about the magazine?' Dolan asked, sliding up in the

bed, sitting up against the wall, wide awake now.

'Carlisle's taken them off the news-stands – '

'Carlisle?'

'Jack Carlisle. I suppose that's who it is. There's not a copy of the *Cosmopolite* left on any news-stand in town – '

'How? What happened?' Dolan said, swinging his feet around, getting to the floor, frowning at Bishop.

'As near as I can get the story it was a regular raid – perfectly timed in the downtown section. A few minutes after the regular deliveries, a couple or three guys visit each news-stand at the same time, grab all the magazines, throw 'em in a car, and beat it.'

'Strong-arm stuff – '

'Several of the news dealers squawked and tried to resist, but the hoods told 'em to shut up or this would only be the beginning. Looks like the old Carlisle technique. He's making damn sure that story about his brother isn't put into circulation – '

'He can't do that!' Dolan exclaimed. 'Heavens – this is the United States of America!'

'Ever hear the old one about the dinge they threw into jail. They couldn't do it – but they did.'

'So – the only magazines out now are the ones in the mail and the ones at the neighbourhood drug-stores – '

'I guess those flying squadrons have even visited the drug-stores by this time. It's after nine o'clock. It wouldn't surprise me if Carlisle had got into the mail and taken those too – '

'I hope to hell he has. Oh, God – how I hope he has! I'd like to see him fool with the government – '

'Funny thing about those guys – they don't care who they fool with – Hell, I been trying to raise you on the phone for two hours, and they said you were out – '

'Yeah,' Dolan said, sitting down, lighting a cigarette, scraping his thumb-nail over his teeth. 'Well – we've got to print

another edition, that's all. The sonofabitch. Who does he think
he is – Hitler – or Mussolini – '

'He is – in a small way. Hell, this country's full of 'em.'

Dolan dragged studiously at his cigarette, scraped his thumb-
nail over his teeth a few more times, and then got up abruptly
and went into the living-room to the telephone. He looked up
Lawrence's home phone number and dialled it. Somebody there
said Mr Lawrence was gone for the evening and wouldn't be
home until around midnight. Dolan went back into the bedroom.

'Lawrence is at a movie or something. If I could get hold of
him I'd make him raise the printers and we'd go right to work
on another edition. God, of all the nights for him to be out – '

'We can do it in the morning. If he'll go for it – '

'What do you mean – if he'll go for it?'

'He's a kind of a weak sister, you know. He's pretty likely to
run for his hole the first sign of trouble – and this is what you
might call trouble. One word from Carlisle and Lawrence'll
fold up like an accordion.'

'We'll make him print it!'

'Not if he doesn't want to, you won't,' Bishop said. 'It's his
plant. My guess is we're up that old creek without a paddle.'

'You think so? – '

'Yeah. Don't get me wrong. I got plenty of guts. But you
might as well look this smack in the face. Carlisle still doesn't
take us too seriously or he wouldn't have been content with just
grabbing all the magazines – '

'By God, that was plenty – '

'Not for him. This is just his characteristic way of warning
you. You'll hear more about this any minute – maybe a visit
from Hitler himself. If he ever goes to Lawrence and tells him
to lay off, you can damn well imagine what will happen – '

The telephone rang. Dolan jumped.

'Get that, will you?' he asked. 'I'm not here – '

Bishop went out to the telephone. Dolan heard him
apologizing and in a minute he came back.

'You're getting up in the world,' he said. 'That was the eminent ex-senator, Mark Fried – '

'Lord!' Dolan exclaimed. 'I'd forgotten I was married – '

'It's a good thing to forget. Your father-in-law wants you to call him. Said no matter what time you got in. By the way, I see you got quite a play in the afternoon papers – '

'I didn't see them. Look, Ed – this is a hell of a spot we're in, isn't it?'

'I'm compelled to admit that it is. Mike, you're delightful. You're the most ingenuous sonofabitch I've ever met. You haven't the faintest idea what you're going to do, have you?'

'I've got one idea – Bud McGonagill. I'm going to get you a special deputy's commission the first thing in the morning, and we're going to put out that magazine if we have to stand guard over the presses. Even if we have to call out the militia to protect the news-stands – '

'That's fine. I'll take the commission, because there are a couple of bastards in this town I'd like to shoot anyway. But don't concern yourself about the militia or the county cops or the city cops. Carlisle bosses the whole works. If we get out this magazine, we'll do it without any help. Personally, I don't think we've got any more chance than a poop in a whirlwind – '

'Maybe I can sell Lawrence on standing pat. I sold him before – '

'But then there wasn't any chance of getting a bomb thrown in the front end of his joint. Now there is. You mark my words, that bastard'll crawl the minute Carlisle opens his mouth. The only way to go about this is to have Carlisle bumped off – '

'There's another way – '

'Yeah, try and find it.'

' – I will. Well . . . I'm going out.'

'Where?'

'Oh – for a ride,' Dolan said, picking up his trench coat and hat, starting out.

'Hey. You better take that along,' Bishop said, pointing to the automatic.

Dolan thought briefly.

'I guess I had,' he said, going back and getting the pistol.

'You'd better be careful where you stick your nose, too,' Bishop said, getting up. 'I wish you'd let me go with you – '

'Come on. I'll be all right,' Dolan said, snapping out the light, walking out, getting into his coat.

They went down the stairs, not saying anything. Bishop's car was parked at the curb, and in the light from the street lamp on the corner Dolan recognized Myra sitting in it. He had the impulse to walk on around the house to the garage to his car and say nothing to her, but he decided there was no sense in causing any more unpleasantness.

'Whyn't you tell me she was down here?' he said to Bishop, walking to the car. ' – Hello, Myra – '

'Hello, Mike – '

'Whyn't you come up?'

'It was all Ed could do to get in,' Myra said, smiling. 'That darky of yours is a pretty faithful watchdog . . . Where're you going on a night like this?'

'. . . For a ride – '

'Mike,' Myra said soberly, 'you're not going to do anything crazy?'

'I'm only going for a ride – '

'Where's he going, Ed?' Myra asked, turning to Bishop, who was inside, under the wheel.

'Search me.'

'Mike, you're not going to fool with Carlisle or anything like that?'

'No – '

'Do you mind if I go with you?'

'I thought you were off me,' Dolan said, in spite of himself.

'This is no time to be childish,' Myra said sharply. 'I'm going with you.'

She pulled at the handle, but Dolan put both hands against the door and pushed, keeping her inside.

'No, you're not,' he said. 'For God's sake, you've got me into enough trouble already. Hadn't been for you I never would have married Lillian – '

'I know it. You cut off your nose to spite your face.'

' – Take her to her flat, Ed. I'll see both of you in the morning – early. Around eight.'

He walked around to the garage and got in his car. As he was backing it out, Walter came down the driveway from Ulysses' room.

'Some guy named Thomas wants you to call him at his home. Said it was very important.'

'I'll bet . . .' Dolan said, continuing to back out.

He drove around in the rain, going nowhere in particular, through streets that were flooded over the curbings, hardly steering the car, thinking it was a shame that the rain was letting up and how swell it would be if it would keep on raining, hard, and that this was the reason the South Sea archipelagos fascinated him so much – the eternal rain; but in the back of his mind was Carlisle – and the *Cosmopolite*, and what a hell of a shape this country was in to permit such things, and that there was a Carlisle in every town in the country, but that millions upon millions were too stupid to care, and that it was that way all over the world: millions upon millions of people who believed Hitler and Mussolini were great fellows, not knowing (or caring) that they were madmen beating on drums, poor diseased bastards, driving a lot of cattle (these same stupid millions upon millions) to slaughter, and that they would surely suck us into it (Hemingway was right about the radio in the next war when he said you can imagine what that will do for hysteria): thinking we should nip all these Carlisles and Hitlers and Mussolinis right now: oh yes, everything is peaches and cream in this superb, marvellous, wonderful paradise called the United States of America, the only country where the radio is free and uncensored, and the press is free and uncensored, and speech is free and uncensored – oh yes, a man can say what he pleases, any time he pleases – the hell he can – you try it, and you get your magazine taken away from you.

> The
> > dirty
> > > goddam
> > > > sonofabitch,

he said to himself, meaning Carlisle (but thinking, too, of Hitler and Mussolini).

... Presently he drove through the great stone arch, the entrance to Weston Park, and then he discovered that he was riding in his car and that this was the section where Lillian lived, his new wife, and he suddenly felt he had been married a long, long time, and he reached for his beard – but knowing there would be no beard. His new wife: well, how do you do, Mrs Michael Dolan, how do you do! Fawncy meeting you here! And who is that distinguished old fluff-duff over there, who sat at the head of the table. I didn't quite catch his name – oh yes, to be sure; to be sure – the Senator. I remember his constructive service in Washington, his distinguished efforts on behalf of his constituents. Well, bah jove, Senator, you're looking fit. Yes, Dolan, Michael Dolan, you remember me, my ancestors came over on the *Mayflower*; oh yes, indeed, the same Dolans, the old kings of grand old Ireland (only now my crest is a crossed pick and shovel beneath a street car rampant); and how do you like this dreadful weather, Senator, you old crooked son of a bitch – and that's a funny one they tell on you, a very funny one (slapping him on the back), that you paid out fifty thousand dollars in Washington to try to get back your wasted powers (whispering in his ear: I read an advertisement in a magazine that might help you); oh, hello, there, darling, there you are, your father and I

were just reminiscing; oh yes, Senator, we'll drive carefully, the
streets certainly are slick; it's really dreadful weather, and thank
you again for that little house you gave us as a wedding present,
it is too, too divoon and the dinner was too, too divoon, and we'll
only play a few rubbers of bridge with the Burlington-Whimseys;
yes, if I see the Count I certainly shall give him your warmest . . .
good night, good night!!!!!

The Negro butler answered the door-bell.

'Is Miss Lillian home?' Dolan asked.

'Come in, sir. Come in,' the butler said affably, opening the
door.

'Are you the boy who let me in this morning?' Dolan asked,
stepping inside.

'I certainly am, Mr Dolan,' the butler said, helping him off
with his coat.

'You seem different – '

'Perhaps it's this black coat, sir. This morning I wore a white
one – '

'No, it's something else. Something about your personality.
You're different – '

'You're different, too, sir,' the Negro said, smiling.

'Oh yes, I realize that. I'm in character now. I've been riding
around for an hour or two getting in character . . . Will you tell
Miss Lillian I'm here – '

'She's expecting you, sir. This way – '

Dolan followed him through the drawing-room into the
library, stopping at the far side of the library door. The Negro
tapped lightly on the door, then stuck his head inside.

'Mr Dolan is here,' he said, and in a moment he stepped
back. 'Go in, Mr Dolan – '

Dolan went inside, and the door was pulled closed behind
him. Dolan looked around curiously. This was a man's den.

'Are you Dolan?' a voice boomed.

'Er – yes. How do you do? You scared me. I didn't see you
behind the chair – '

'I just wanted to be sure. I'm Lillian's father.'

'I know. I recognized you from your pictures, Senator. But I thought the boy said Lillian was expecting – '

'I told him to say that. I wanted to be sure I got to see you in case you did come. Sit down – '

'Isn't she here?'

'I don't think she wants to see you – '

'In that case there's no point in staying,' Dolan said, turning to go.

'Sit down,' the Senator said, using his cigar for a pointer. Dolan sat down.

'How'd all this happen – this marriage?'

'Well – it simply happened, that's all – '

'Why?'

'For the most obvious reason in the world, my dear Senator – we are very fond of each other.'

'Crap,' the Senator snorted, walking around in a small half-circle, fiddling with his cigar, acting like a district-attorney in a court-room. 'I'm going to tell you something that may surprise you, Dolan. I've heard about you before. Fred Coughlin told me all about you. Did you know that when you were having that affair with his daughter he had a private detective trailing you for several weeks?'

'Not weeks – about ten days,' Dolan said slowly. 'Peculiar thing, too. All my friends kept telling me some guy had been asking them all sorts of embarrassing questions. Well, one day I called up three or four of my pals and told them that sooner or later some guy would come in and start asking about me, and when he did I wanted them to phone me at the office.

'I went to the Detective Bureau and talked to Inspector Trushka about it, and Trushka promised to help me. I used to be a police reporter years ago, and I gave Trushka favourable publicity from time to time – as a matter of fact I practically made him an Inspector, single-handed – '

'Never mind, Dolan,' the Senator said.

'I hate to bore you, Senator, but this story has got a point. Trushka promised to have a couple of dicks stand by for a phone call from me – and a couple days later I got the flash that this guy who was asking all the questions was in the office of a friend of mine. I phoned Trushka and the two dicks met me there. We picked the guy up and took him to police head- quarters. He admitted being a private dick, but he would admit nothing else.

'Well, the coppers don't particularly care for private dicks at best, so we took this fellow to a little room down in the base- ment. A sound-proof room, Senator, with only one chair – a replica of an electric chair – in the middle, with a big spotlight shining in the face of whoever sits in it. We strapped this fellow in and bruised him up a little, but still he wouldn't talk. So we went to work on him with the rubber hose – and a couple of hours later he admitted that Fred Coughlin had hired him.

'I thought this was a little out of line, because Coughlin was no angel himself, so I hung around for a couple of weeks wait- ing to nail him. Oh yes, I forgot to tell you that I used to be nuts about miniature camera work – you know, the candid cameras. Well, my agents tipped me off one night that he was at a certain hotel in a certain room with a young girl – he likes 'em young, the high-school age, so I went up in the corridor and hid in the maid's closet until he came out. You won't believe that he was dumb enough to come out with the girl, instead of leaving her behind, but he did, and I got a swell flash-lamp picture of them together. I've got the negative in the safe- deposit vault. I'll print it up some time if you're interested. I sent Coughlin a print – and since then he's been all right.

'So – that's rather a long answer to a simple question, but it clears up the doubt in your mind about the private detective.'

'Very interesting,' the Senator said. ' – Were you in love with Coughlin's daughter?'

'Come, come, my dear Senator – let's not rake up the past. We are concerned only with the present – '

'Stop being dramatic, Dolan, and tell me what you intend doing about Lillian – '

'I'd like to talk that over with Lillian first – Do you mind if I smoke?'

'Go ahead, go ahead. Of course, you know this marriage is positively impossible. Are you going to rectify it – or am I going to have to take action myself?'

'What action could you possibly take – Senator?' Dolan asked, lighting a cigarette. 'Lillian is my wife – '

'Not yet, she isn't. I could have it annulled.'

'On what grounds?'

'That she isn't really your wife. That you've – er – never slept with her.'

'Oh, let's not be stupid about this, Senator. You know very well the only way to get an annulment is for me to subscribe to it. You can't take this thing into court. I don't want it to go into court.'

'Well, you don't think for one moment that you're in love with Lillian, do you?'

'That I wouldn't know. She's beautiful and nice – and I'm very fond of her. But love – I wouldn't know.'

'Of course,' the Senator said grimly, 'I could have this remedied myself – but that would be messy – and I hate violence – '

'Now cut out the dramatics, Senator. You could, but you won't – '

The Senator wrinkled his forehead, thinking.

'Look here,' he said finally. 'I want to break this up and send Lillian away to Europe for a year or two. I appeal to your sportsmanship to give her up without a scandal.'

'You touch me in a tender spot, Senator. I've always been a good sportsman, but lately I've learned that there's no such word in the bright lexicon of success, if you don't mind the trite phrase. It's a game of dog eat dog. You ought to know that. You've been through the mill.'

'What will induce you to give her up?'

'It seems to me you're assuming a lot of things. Admitting I don't love her – but am fond of her – how do you know she doesn't love me?'

The Senator did not answer, walking rapidly to the bell-cord, pulling it, and then turned facing the door, smiling as if he had been waiting for this opportunity.

The Negro came in.

'Ask Miss Lillian to step in here – '

The Negro stepped back, the suggestion of a smile on his face, and Lillian came in. She evidently had been waiting in the library. Dolan was surprised. He wondered how much of the conversation she had overheard.

'Hello, Lillian,' he said, getting up, putting out his cigarette.

'Hello – well, father, dear – '

'I think if you'll tell Mr Dolan what you told me tonight, I can arrange this – '

'Tell him about what, Daddy?'

'About your not loving him – '

'Oh,' Lillian said, turning to Dolan. 'What Daddy says is true. I don't love you – '

'Who decided you didn't love me – you or he?'

'Oh, I decided. You really didn't take me seriously, did you?' she asked innocently.

' – For a minute I did,' Dolan said, laughing. 'Yes, you certainly fooled me – '

'I just did it for the fun of it,' Lillian said, 'I didn't think you'd take me seriously – '

'That's all, Lillian,' the Senator said. 'You may go now – '

'Good night,' Lillian said.

'Good night,' Dolan called. ' – Marvellous sense of humour,' he said to the Senator, when she had gone.

'Well – you see I was right.'

'Yes, you were. I don't think she loves me – '

'Of course, she doesn't. And you don't want to be married to a girl who doesn't love you, do you? Of course you don't! Now will you agree that an annulment is the best way?'

'Absolutely,' Dolan said. 'Absolutely.'

'Fine!' the Senator said, rubbing his hands briskly, rolling the cigar around in his mouth. 'You know Oppenheimer in the bank building?'

'Yes – '

'He's my lawyer. You meet me there at ten o'clock tomorrow morning and he'll have the papers ready.'

'I'll be there,' Dolan said. 'Well – '

'My boy,' the Senator said, beaming, shaking Dolan's hand. 'You're very sensible – Come, I'll take you to the door – '

'Thanks, Senator,' Dolan said. 'There's only one thing you've overlooked.'

The Senator frowned.

'I've got something you want – and you've got something I want. That's a pretty good premise for making a deal, isn't it?'

'I don't quite see what you're driving at – '

'The fact is, Senator, I'm rather badly in need of money – '

Every muscle in Mark Fried's body locked, and he stood staring from beneath his bushy eyebrows.

'I need this money to carry on a sort of business I'm in – and I thought probably you might help me.'

'A shakedown, eh? A deliberate shakedown – '

'Not deliberate. The idea only occurred to me a minute ago. When Lillian made it so plain she didn't love me. You remember – when she said she only got married for the fun of it. I came out here to call off the whole thing, and now I find Lillian had fun. That'll cost you – '

'I won't give you a goddam penny!'

'No dough,' Dolan said mildly, 'no annulment.'

'I'll have you fixed for this. I'll have you taken care of, you goddam blackmailing Irisher!'

'Not blackmail, Senator – business. I need money and you've got money. I want fifty thousand dollars.'

'Fifty thou – '

'I'm not going to argue. Fifty G's.'

'Why, why – ' the Senator sputtered.

' – I'll give you twenty-five – ' he snapped.

'Thirty-seven five – '

'Thirty-five. Yes or no?'

' – Yes. I'll meet you at ten o'clock tomorrow morning in Oppenheimer's office – Don't bother, Senator. I can find the door – '

Cully, the foreman of the mechanical department, was a little dubious about printing another run of the *Cosmopolite*. Yes, he had heard about what happened to the magazines last night, and he thought it was a damned shame, too, but then he had a schedule to maintain, and today was the day he had to print and bind the monthly magazine of that insurance company, and that would take most of the day. Anything that interfered with that would delay everything and send the men into overtime, and then Lawrence would really hit the ceiling.

'I'll take full responsibility,' Dolan said.

'I know, Mike – but I'd rather Mr Lawrence okayed it.'

'But I've told you Lawrence isn't home. They said he had left for the office.'

'He ought to be here by now – '

'I know he ought, but he isn't – and he may not come in for an hour. I don't want to lose any more time. Look, Cully – all that type's still in the formes, isn't it?'

'Yes – it's still in the formes all right – '

'Then what the hell. Stick 'em on the machines and have at it. What was the press run yesterday?'

'Twenty-two something – '

'Make this one thirty-five hundred.'

'It's going to gum up my schedule – '

'Well, if the other job goes into overtime, I'll pay it. Now, have at it, will you?'

'All right, Mike – but if Lawrence says anything – '

'I'll take care of that. Just bear down – '

'Hi, Cully – '

'Hello, Ed – '

'What about it?' Bishop asked Dolan.

'Okay. Let's get out of here and let Cully go to work,' Dolan said, walking out of the press-room into the corridor. 'See Bud?'

'Yeah. Look,' he said, showing the deputy sheriff's badge. 'This is kind of cheap looking. Bud's got one with a diamond in it – given him by the Elks or Moose or something. Ten minutes more and I'd had that one.'

'Did he give you a gun?'

'No, he loaned me one. Police Positive thirty-eight. Says he got it off Pretty Boy Floyd that time he picked him out here – but I think he's a goddam liar.'

'Bud likes to impress people with the big-time criminals he's known.'

'I know. Good guy, though – '

They entered the office.

'Did you get it?' Myra asked.

Bishop nodded, lifted the tail of his coat so she could see the pistol in his hip pocket.

'Badge, holster – everything. Guess where I was sworn in – '

'Where?' Dolan said.

'In the lavatory of the barber shop across the street. Bud said he had to be careful. Imagine it – a can! Symbolic, what?' he said, laughing.

'What about Cully?' Myra asked Dolan.

The dull rattling roll of the press came over.

'That the *Cosmopolite*?' Myra asked.

'Yes – '

'Swell! Extra swell! We'll show that bastard where he gets off!'

'What about the news-stands?' Bishop asked. 'Carlisle strong-armed 'em once, he'll do it again.'

'Will he?' Dolan said, walking over to the back window, motioning them to follow. 'Take a look at that – '

In the parking lot in the rear of the plant, under the roof of the open shed where Lawrence left his trucks, were seven or eight men standing around.

'Gorillas,' Dolan said. 'Mugs.   They speak Carlisle's language. Know where I got 'em? Out of the police department's Peerage. Emmett corralled 'em for me.'

'When did you see Emmett?' Bishop asked, surprised.

'This morning. Six o'clock this morning. I went to his home. I explained what had happened and told him I needed some help – and there they are. I'd like to see somebody try to strong-arm those babies – '

'Well, I'll be a sonofabitch if he didn't go to the chief of police to get help,' Bishop said, slapping Dolan on the back. 'When did you think of this?'

'Last night when I took that ride neither one of you wanted me to take. That wasn't all I thought of either – '

'What?' they asked.

'It's not in the bag yet, but if it goes through, our worries are over.'

'Money?' Bishop asked. 'It is money. From whom?'

'Fried – '

'Oh, so that's where you went last night,' Myra said. 'What happened?'

'Stop bawling me out,' Dolan said, turning to Bishop to explain to him. 'I was riding around last night thinking about a lot of things and wound up at Lillian's. I don't know why I went there or anything. I didn't start out with the idea of going there – but bang! and there I was.'

'And I suppose she fell right into your arms – ' Myra said.

'Shut up,' Dolan said, over his shoulder. 'Well, the upshot of the whole thing was that she said she only married me for the fun of it and that she didn't love me – '

'The old man ribbed her into saying that – '

'Sure, he did. He was there when all this happened. He called her in as Exhibit A to prove I should have the marriage annulled. She thought it was a hell of a swell joke.'

'It must have been funny, at that,' Bishop said. 'Go on – '

'That's all. I said okay, we'll have the thing annulled. Only – I wanted fifty thousand bucks to do it – '

'God!' Bishop said, whistling. 'Fifty thousand! Did you get it?'

'I settled for thirty-five. I'm meeting Fried this morning at his lawyer's office to sign the papers – '

'Hell, you're a wizard,' Bishop said, shaking his head. 'That thirty-five and the four grand we've got in Myra's name'll put out a lot of magazines. Maybe I could get a couple of hundred advance, you know, the kid being down – '

'Sure, sure, Ed. Look. All right I worried – '

'Why, for God's sake! Your worries are over. You've got nothing to worry about – '

'That money Fried promised me. I feel like a heel – '

'Will you listen to the guy?' Bishop said to Myra. 'Look here, Mike. You're entitled to that dough. For God's sake, will you ever get it through your head that the guy with scruples nowadays is always the guy who gets screwed? Besides, that money is going to a worthy cause – '

'You mean the magazine. Sure, that's what I thought,' Dolan said soberly. 'That's exactly why I made him the proposition. What do you think, Myra?' he asked, walking over to the desk where Myra was standing, chewing on a pencil.

'I think you're goddam lucky he didn't break your neck,' Myra said.

'Oh, so you think I'm a heel,' Dolan said, quietly. 'I ought to bust you in the nose so's not to let you think I mind!'

'You know why you're so suddenly sore, don't you?' Myra said quietly. 'You really do know, don't you?'

'I ought to smack you one for luck – knock some of that sarcasm out of you – '

'Lay off, you two,' Bishop growled, coming around between them. 'Never did I see anything like it. One of these days I won't be here when you start snapping, and then what'll happen? Lay off – '

Dolan growled in his throat, something unintelligible, and Bishop moved from between them towards the front window.

' – Mike,' he called softly . . .

Dolan caught an ominous quality in the tone and moved swiftly behind him, looking over his shoulder.

A man had just emerged from the office and was crossing the street. He was a small man, unimpressive from the rear. They watched him cross the street and take up a position waiting for a trolley-car. When he finally turned, facing the building, both Bishop and Dolan stepped quickly away from the window so he could not see them.

'Funny he didn't come up to see us,' Dolan said.

'No, it's not. He doesn't think we're important enough – '

'Who is it?' Myra asked.

'Jack Carlisle,' Dolan said, biting his lip.

Myra crossed quickly to the window to take a look.

'Don't let him see you looking,' Dolan said.

'I'm not,' she said, easing her head along the wall, peeping out the window. 'He's not looking this way . . . so that's the local dictator! Well . . .' she said, coming away from the window, 'the sight of him explains a number of questions I've been puzzled about – '

The dull clatter of the press, that had furnished an undertone for their conversation, suddenly stopped.

Dolan and Bishop looked at each other.

'Come on,' Dolan said.

He rushed downstairs with Bishop behind him and went into Lawrence's office without knocking. Lawrence was just taking off his raincoat.

'Did you stop that press?' Dolan asked.

'Yes – and I'll stop it again if it's ever started without my approval,' Lawrence said, coming back to his desk. 'By what right do you give orders here?'

'I tried to get you and couldn't – and I was anxious to get a re-run of the magazine,' Dolan said. 'Why? What's so wrong with that?'

'You know very well that today is the day we put out the insurance house-organ. We've had that contract too long to violate it now.'

'That's not the reason,' Bishop said.

'Wait a minute, Ed,' Dolan said. 'Jack Carlisle's visit here wouldn't have anything to do with stopping the press, would it?'

'Carlisle – Carlisle . . .'

'Stop stalling. I just saw him cross the street – '

'Mr Carlisle was here,' Lawrence admitted. 'He suggested that it might be – '

'He didn't suggested anything. He ordered it. Well, all right. What about it? Are you going to let him intimidate you?'

'It's not intimidation – it's that I wouldn't want to be drawn into a libel suit. I told you when I read the article that I thought – '

'Answer my question – do you print this magazine or don't you?'

'Well, Dolan, it's like this – '

'I told you he was yellow,' Bishop said. 'I told you he'd crawl – '

'Okay,' Dolan said. 'I'll print it somewhere else. I'll take what's been run off so far and the formes, and I'll do it some-where else. No objection, is there?'

'Why, certainly not,' Lawrence said, relieved.

'That's what's wrong with this country,' Bishop said, leaning over the desk. 'A lot of gutless little squirts like you, you bastard – '

'Come on,' Dolan said.

They went into the press-room. There was a stack of magazine sheets on the cutting machine and another stack on the table, where the girls were folding and binding them. Cully came up to them, looking doleful.

'Well,' he said.

'We're moving,' Dolan said. 'I'll have a truck here in a few minutes, and we'll take what's been done. Formes too.'

'Sorry, Mike,' Cully said. 'Tough business bucking Jack Carlisle – '

'It's beginning to look like it, all right,' Dolan said. 'Will you get everything together and let those guys out in back have it – you know, those mugs – '

'Sure – '

'Thanks for everything, Cully.'

They went back upstairs. Myra was emptying the drawers of the desk, stacking the stuff on the desk.

'We're moving,' Bishop said.

'I suspected as much when the press stopped – '

'Ed,' Dolan said, picking up his coat, 'stick here until I get back. I've got to see that lawyer, and then I'll get a truck.'

'Where're we moving?'

'If I don't get that money, we're not moving anywhere – we're finished. If I do get it . . . Just stick here. I'll speak to those guys out back. You think I'd better send them up?'

'What for?'

'In case anything should happen – '

'They'd only be in the way. Myra and I and old Pretty Boy Floyd here can handle things,' he said, patting his hip.

'And Thomas just called,' Myra said.

'I wish he'd let me alone,' Dolan said, moving to the door.

'Mike,' Myra called, 'do be careful – '

'I will . . .'

Oppenheimer, the lawyer, walked slowly up and down his

carpet, hands in his pockets, looking alternately from Dolan to the window.

'I think the rain's just about over now,' he remarked. 'Looks like it's breaking up in the north. If we get a wind it'll be dry enough by tomorrow afternoon to play golf. You play golf, Dolan?'

'No, I never got around to it – '

'Great game, golf.'

'So they tell me – '

Oppenheimer stopped in front of Dolan, looking down at him.

'I don't think you handled this thing very wisely, Dolan. The Senator's not the kind of a man you should offend. I know him. He's very much upset.'

'I'm upset too – '

'You should have taken his cheque. You practically insulted him by refusing it.'

'Look, Mr Oppenheimer. I came here to sign that waiver, and I will sign it when he comes back with the cash. I refused his cheque simply because I'm not going to take chances on him having the payment stopped – '

'But that's why he was offended. That was tantamount to saying you didn't trust him. The Senator is an honourable man – '

'I know, I know. I know all about the Senator. You forget I worked on a newspaper for several years – '

The door opened.

'Well, well, come in, Senator,' Oppenheimer said.

'Here,' the Senator said, tossing a bundle of currency into Dolan's lap. 'Seventy five hundred dollar bills. Now, by God, you sign that waiver or I'll personally throw you out the window – '

'Thanks,' Dolan said, getting up, going to the desk. 'Where do I sign, Mr Oppenheimer?'

'Right there – right there – '

Dolan signed his name and straightened up.

'Thanks,' he said again, putting the money in his inside pocket, walking out.

The secretary pushed her head inside the door.

'I hate to interrupt, Mr Baumgarten,' she said, 'but you're due at Pacific Press at eleven, and it's ten-thirty now – '

'All right,' Baumgarten said. 'I'll be there.'

The secretary's head disappeared, and the door closed again.

'They're installing some machinery,' he said to Dolan. 'What was all that you were trying to tell me?'

'I'm putting out a magazine,' Dolan began patiently.

'I know. The *Cosmopolite*. I know that. What were you saying about the press?'

'You sold Lawrence his machinery, didn't you?'

'Yes.'

'That's what I wanted to know. I'm not printing the magazine there any more. I've got the formes and everything, and I simply wanted to know if you could tell me where there is a press in town exactly like his.'

'You want to put out the magazine somewhere else – '

'Right. But I want to keep the same size.'

'There are several presses in town like Lawrence's. Green has one – '

'He's out. His uncle publishes the *Courier*, and sooner or later – No, he's out.'

'Grissom has one, right around the corner. Used to do a lot of house organs and mining brochures. I sold him some new equipment a couple of months ago.'

'You think he might take on the *Cosmopolite*?'

'I don't see why not. He's your best chance, anyway. Of course, it won't help your standing in the community much to be associated with him – '

'I can't be choosey, I've got to take what I can get. Why wouldn't it help my standing?'

'He's the fellow who used to print those Communistic tracts. That's why Lawrence does most of the house-organ business today, too – '

'Apparently it didn't hurt your standing in the community to associate with him. I thought you were pretty active in the American Legion – '

'Business is business,' Baumgarten said. 'I only belong to the Legion at night.'

' – Grissom, you say?'

'Right around the corner. I'd take you there except that I'm pressed for time.'

'That's all right. Thanks, Henry – '

'Okay, Mike. Let me know how you come out – '

Grissom was a mild-looking man of fifty-odd, white-haired, with blue eyes and a scholarly face. He was very much interested in Dolan's proposition. He kept nodding his head and smiling through the story of what had happened to the *Cosmopolite*, and when Dolan brought it up to date by relating how Lawrence had stopped the press a few hours ago, Grissom laughed heartily, very much amused.

'Well, Mr Dolan,' he said, 'you need have no fears about this press being stopped. At the risk of being considered irreverent, I want you to know I am not in the least awed by Jack Carlisle.'

'Have you got a place here we could use as an office?'

'That. Would that do?'

He pointed to the rear of the plant to a balcony.

'My proof-readers used to use that – when I had proof-readers. How big is your staff? Or do you have a staff?'

'Three. Two others and myself – '

'I don't see why you couldn't use the balcony – '

'That's not important, anyway. The important thing is, when can we finish the press run?'

'Any time. I could start now if I had the formes. I'll have to get some girls who know how to fold and bind – '

'We can do that ourselves – if we have to. Here,' Dolan said, putting his hand in his inside pocket, working a bill loose with his fingers. 'Here's five hundred dollars. Just to prove there's no monkey business about this – '

'Why – this isn't necessary – '

'Take it – '

'Well . . .' Grissom said, taking the bill, still surprised.

'I'll get a truck and bring the stuff down. Be here in an hour. I'd like to get started by noon if I could – '

'I'll rustle up a crew,' Grissom said . . .

Thirty minutes later Dolan arrived at the parking lot of the Lawrence plant in a moving van. All the formes and bound and unbound leaves of the magazine were outside on a work bench, neatly stacked, being watched by the gorillas the police chief had rounded up for him.

'Load that stuff on the truck, fellows – and after that we have some lunch. We're moving down to the wholesale district, and some time this afternoon we'll have the magazine ready to be delivered.'

He walked around to the front of the building and went upstairs.

'Well?' Bishop and Myra said.

Dolan took out the currency and laid it on the desk.

'Thirty-four thousand, five hundred dollars. Cash.'

'Well, I'll be a sonofabitch,' Bishop exclaimed, picking up the money, riffling it. 'This is the most dough I ever saw at one time in my life.'

'What about the magazine? Where're we going? I see you brought a truck big enough to move the entire joint,' Myra said.

'I found a place on Sixth Avenue, just off Terminal. Man by the name of Grissom – '

'Grissom?' Bishop said suddenly.

'You know him?'

'I know who he is. He's radical. The cops have run him in a couple of times – '

'He seemed harmless enough to me. Very nice and very inoffensive. I don't care whether he's radical or not. He's got a printing-press, and that's all I'm interested in – '

' – Okay. I'm game,' Bishop said. 'But I can tell you right now I don't have to be a crystal-gazer to know what's going to happen – '

'The first thing that's happening is, Myra and I are going to the bank. You go down on the truck with the stuff, and we'll meet you there as soon as we can.'

'You don't mean you're going to deposit all this money in my name, do you?' Myra said, taking the bundle of currency from Bishop.

'I can't very well put it in my own – not with all the judgements and things I've got against me,' Dolan said. 'That's as good as they want – me to have dough in the bank. They'd slap an attachment on it so fast it'd make your head swim.'

'See you at Grissom's,' Bishop said.

'Sure. Come on, Myra – '

'You'd better call Thomas,' Myra said, putting on her hat. 'He's tried to get you a couple of times – '

'It's beginning to look like the guy's queer for me,' Dolan said. 'Come on, let's get that money in the bank before somebody hijacks us – '

Vol. i. No. 5 of the *Cosmopolite* was back on the news-stands shortly before five o'clock that afternoon, in plenty of time to catch the home-going traffic. Big posters read:

ON SALE HERE
THE COSMOPOLITE
The Magazine They Tried to Suppress
In This Issue:
THE INSIDE STORY OF DR HARRY CARLISLE
The Cosmopolite
(*The Truth, the Whole Truth, and Nothing but the Truth*)

At each of seven important stands in the heaviest traffic centres, beside the pile of magazines, stood one of the gorillas. Each man had been equipped with a leather black-jack and a pair of brass knuks (that Dolan had bought from a pawnshop), and was keeping an eye out for trouble. They had been fully rehearsed and knew what to do if any attempt was made at further strong-arming.

Dolan, Bishop, and Myra cruised around these seven stands, reconnoitring, checking up, giving each gorilla a ten-dollar bill, and promising him another ten if he protected the magazines until nine o'clock.

'Swell. They're going like hotcakes,' Dolan said, as he drove away from the last news-stand. 'And not even a chirp from Carlisle.'

'Let's don't get premature,' Bishop said. 'There's plenty of time left for him to start something – '

'Those mugs'll know what to do. They love it. Three of 'em used to work for Bergoff.'

'Who's Bergoff?'

'Pearl Bergoff. You never heard of Pearl Bergoff?'

'I think I do remember something about him,' Bishop said. 'Story in *Fortune*, wasn't there?'

'That's right – '

'Mike,' Myra said, 'you'd better get in touch with McGonagill about that girl who used to work in Carlisle's office. You're going to need her. It's a cinch the Grand Jury will want to know about this now, and the Medical Association – '

'I'm going to call him tonight. Oh, I'll have my facts straight, don't you worry – '

He was stopped by a traffic semaphore.

' – Look,' Bishop said quietly. 'In that car to your left – '

Dolan looked. An expensive sedan had pulled alongside. A man was driving, with a woman sitting beside him. The woman was reading aloud from the *Cosmopolite*. The man had his head slanted over so he could hear.

'Get it?' Bishop asked.

'It'll be all over town by tonight.'

'It's all over town now,' Bishop said.

The semaphore changed and Dolan drove on, south, towards the ocean.

'Where're we going to eat? . . .' Myra asked.

'My God,' Bishop said. 'You're not hungry again?'

'I could eat a dead Confederate soldier,' she said.

'Want to go to the beach?' Dolan asked. 'You like clam chowder?'

'I like good clam chowder, but I've never had any at a beach yet. It's too close to the ocean.'

'Clams come out of the ocean, you dope,' Dolan said.

'I know it. That's what I mean – '

'I'll go for anything but hamburgers,' Bishop said. 'Now that we're in the money I never want to see another hamburger again.'

'Myra,' Dolan said, 'remind me to take a cheque to David and Mrs Marsden tonight – '

'Why, for God's sake?' Bishop asked. 'We may need that dough. You don't have to pay them yet – '

'I'm going to while I've got it. I'm going to pay up some other bills, too. I just thought of something,' he said, laughing, pushing down on the foot accelerator, anxious to get to the beach and have dinner and then get back home.

The telephone rang, and a few minutes later Ulysses came into the room.

'That was Mr McGonagill. He said you'd know what it was about.'

Dolan got up off the bed and started out.

'He's hung up,' Ulysses said, stopping him.

'Whyn't you call me?' Dolan said crossly. 'You know I wanted to talk to him – '

'No, sir, I didn't. You said you didn't want to talk to nobody. Didn't he, Miss Myra?'

'That's right, Ulysses. It's not his fault, Mike,' she said. 'He's done nothing but answer that telephone since eight o'clock.'

'I'm sorry, Ulysses,' Dolan said. 'I'll call him at home.'

He went into the living-room and called McGonagill at home.

'Bud? . . . This is Mike Dolan. You want me? . . . Swell! What is it? . . . Wait a moment, let me get a pencil and write it down . . . All right. Jean Christie. Where does she live? . . . Dolly Madison Apartments. Good . . . Oh, you did? Swell, Bud – I appreciate this a lot. Say, hear anything from Carlisle? . . . You didn't, hunh? We put out the magazines this afternoon . . . You did? What'd you think of the story? . . . I'll say it's hot stuff. Thanks, Bud – thanks very much – '

He went back into the living-room.

'McGonagill's located the girl for us. Name's Jean Christie, and she lives at the Dolly Madison Apartments. What's more, he's talked to her, and she says she'll be glad to testify if they ever call on her.'

'By God, that's marvellous,' Bishop said.

'He said we'd better slip her fifty – just for her time, you know. That's all right – '

Myra lay down on the bed, very pale, and started fanning herself with a book.

'What's the matter?' Dolan asked, a little alarmed.

'Those clams – they're riding my stomach with spurs,' she said. 'I knew it – I knew it.'

'You want anything?'

'No, I'll be all right in a minute,' she said, groaning.

'Ed,' Dolan said, 'I think I'll run over and have a talk with this Christie girl – '

'Go ahead if you want to, but I don't see much sense in it. If Bud spoke to her we've got nothing to worry about.'

'Just the same I'd feel better if I had a talk with her myself . . . You sure you don't want anything, Myra? Can I bring you something from the drug-store?'

'I'm all right,' Myra said. 'But don't be gone too long, will you? Ed, hadn't you better go with him?'

'You stay here, Ed,' Dolan said. 'I won't be gone long . . .'

'I'm sorry I couldn't ask you to my room,' Jean Christie said, 'but this is a women's apartment and they've got old-fashioned ideas.'

'This lounge is all right,' Dolan said. 'Thank you for coming down.'

'Not at all. I was expecting you. Mr McGonagill said you'd probably call – '

'I understand he told you what I wanted.'

'He did. About the Harry Carlisle story in your magazine.'

'Have you seen the magazine?'

'That part of it I've read, yes. You certainly spoke right out, didn't you?'

'That's about the only way to handle a story like that – right on the nose. Do you remember either the Griffith or McAlister girl?'

'Both of them. I assisted in both operations. The McAlister girl died in my arms.'

'She did?' Dolan exclaimed, astonished. 'God, I never thought getting the goods on Carlisle'd be this simple. Miss Christie, I'm afraid there'll be an investigation about this, and I wonder if you'd – well – '

'Tell my story to the Grand Jury?'

'Would you? – I hate to ask you, but unless we can get evidence we won't have a leg to stand on – '

'I'll tell it, you can just bet I'll tell it,' she said, with vehemence. 'That's not all I'll tell, either. He performed a criminal operation on me, too. He got me, in that condition himself and operated on me – and then he fired me a month later.'

'I don't blame you for being sore at him,' Dolan said. 'You've got a squawk coming. But I would think he'd be too smart to offend you – '

'You would think so, wouldn't you? Perhaps it's my fault, perhaps I used the wrong technique. I used to plead with him – and, of course, that invariably makes a man despise a woman. Then, too, he has always depended on his brother's power to get him out of any jam. He thought he had me bluffed. Believe me, Mr Dolan – I've been praying for a chance like this – a chance to get even – '

'Here it is. I'll tell you what I think. I think we would be smart to go to a notary public right now and get your sworn statement. I know a notary who'd take it. Would you mind?'

'Whatever you think. I've got to be back in by eleven o'clock – '

'I think yes. It can't do any harm. I'd feel much better about it.'

'All right. I'll get my things.'

'Here,' Dolan said, handing her an envelope as she got up, an envelope with fifty dollars in it.

'What is this?' she asked, blushing, knowing what it was.

'A note. Open it upstairs. I'll wait for you right here . . .'

She smiled at him, moving towards the elevator.

There were three mugs sticking to the ceiling, face downward, with long pieces of lead pipe in their hands. They wore white gauze helmets and red rubber gloves, and they were all looking down at Dolan, whispering. In a moment they started swinging the lead pipes at his head, not angry at all, but smiling and laughing like kids playing a game. Dolan tried to ward off the blows, tried to get up, but found he could move only in an absurdly slow slow-motion. The pipes crashed into his head and he thought: Hell, why can't I move? and finally he fell out of bed and started crawling, with them directly behind him swinging those lead pipes. He finally managed to get to his feet, but his legs were working in that absurdly slow slow-motion too, and he leaned over, bending almost double, putting his hands on the ground, shoving with them, trying desperately to increase his speed. The three mugs kept banging at him with those lead pipes . . . and he screamed and sat up, opening his eyes.

'Quiet, quiet, stop fighting,' Bishop was saying.

For a moment Dolan thought he had gone crazy. The sun was shining in the window, a perfectly visible rectangle of heat. A minute ago it was dark and now it was light.

'Lie down,' Bishop was saying, pushing him gently back against the pillow, him

fighting

fighting

fighting

to figure out what the hell was going on. He touched the pillow with the back of his head and groaned, feeling as if a kettle of hot water had been turned over on his forehead. But now that he was below the rectangle of sunlight, and was no longer blinded by it, he could see he was in his own room. And there was Bishop, looking haggard and worn, and Myra, standing beside him, looking a little haggard and worn, too. My God, he thought vaguely, I've been hurt, and then BANG! the wall in his mind that was keeping him from remembering broke and shattered, and it was all very plain: he had taken Jean Christie back to her hotel after getting the deposition, and was just getting out of his car in the garage when three mugs . . .

'Jesus!' Dolan said. 'How badly am I hurt?'

'Not as badly as you might have been,' Bishop said, sitting down on the bed, smiling. 'You're a lucky Mick – my God, what a skull you must have!'

'It hurts like hell,' Dolan said, running his hand over the heavy bandage. 'Hell, I never had a chance. They slugged me before I could turn around.'

'I can't understand why the hell you didn't yell,' Myra said. 'We didn't know anything about it until we heard the struggle.

When we got down they were running across the lot – '

'I took six shots at 'em,' Bishop said. 'I was so goddam excited I didn't even come close – '

'Carlisle, hunh?' Dolan said, biting his lip.

'Well, it certainly wasn't any pal – that's a cinch. What happened? Feel like talking?'

'I'm all right. What's the matter with my head?'

'Nothing but a couple of gashes. They took a few stitches. What happened with the Christie girl?'

'Marvellous. Harry Carlisle had even operated on her. With her as a witness we can send him up for life. I got her deposition – '

'You did? Where is it?'

'Crammed down behind the seat of my car. Run down and get it – '

'I'll say I will!' Bishop said, walking out rapidly.

'How'd you happen not to have it in your pocket?' Myra asked.

'A hunch – a pure hunch.'

'It's a good thing. Those bastards took everything you had. They must have been experts at their trade. We got down there within a minute or two after we saw what was going on, and there you were on the ground, your pockets wrong-side out. I wonder if Carlisle knew you were with that girl – '

'I don't think so. Those guys didn't go through my pockets looking for anything in particular. They were just making sure – How badly is my head hurt? Hand me a mirror – '

'Just a few stitches, that's all – '

'It can't be hurt much, because I can think and talk and remember everything that happened. It's sore as hell, though – '

'Naturally. Be quiet, Mike – '

'I'm all right. What the hell, can't I talk? I'm all right.'

'Stop acting and be still – '

'I'm not acting. Goddam it, why do you always think I'm acting? Why do you think I'm always being heroic? Goddam it,' he said, sitting up, swinging his feet to the floor, standing up. 'See there, wise guy? I'm not even wobbly.'

'Go ahead and fall and break your goddam neck and see if I care – '

Dolan snorted, walking across to the mirror over the bureau. There was a long scratch on his face and his head was heavily bandaged. He cocked his head from side to side, looking in the mirror, and then turned around, smiling.

'Even in this turban I'm still the best-looking guy in this town, and what do you think of that?'

'Not in that rig, you're not. Mike, will you please get back into bed?'

He looked down and discovered he had on his pyjama coat but not the pants.

'Who undressed me?'

'Ed and I – '

'And as usual you got it backwards. I sleep in pants but no coat. Remember that in the future. Throw me that robe.'

Myra threw him the bathrobe and he put it on.

'Didn't you ever get anything right?' he asked.

'For God's sake, get back into bed,' Bishop said, disgusted, coming into the room.

'Find it?' Dolan asked.

'I've been reading it on the way up. Fine addenda for your collection of erotica.'

'Every word of it's the truth – '

'That doesn't keep it from being erotic. Listen to this, Myra – '

'You needn't. I can imagine,' Myra said. 'Don't you think we ought to put that affidavit in a safe place?' she asked Mike. 'Don't you think it ought to go in your safety deposit vault?'

'I guess so. Hell, I hate to go to town with this mess on my head. I'll have to answer a million goofy questions – '

'You're not going to town. You're staying here,' Bishop said.

'The hell I am! Scram, and let me get dressed.'

Bishop looked at Myra.

'No use trying to argue with him. He wouldn't miss this opportunity for the world. He delights in being the superman, you know . . .'

'What happened to you?' Grissom asked Dolan, as the three of them walked in.

'I got man-handled – '

'They even swiped his pistol and badge,' Myra said.

'Carlisle?' Grissom asked, not paying any attention to her.

'I suppose so – '

'Certainly. Who else?' Bishop said.

'You bounce when you hit,' Grissom said, shaking his head. 'You've got guts, Dolan – '

'Go on, Dolan – admit it. Just once,' Myra said.

Dolan glared at her.

'Where'd it happen?' Grissom asked.

'At my garage. Three or four mugs slugged me when I was getting out of the car.'

'Well, don't you think you should stay home and take it easy?'

'I wouldn't give the sonofabitch that much satisfaction – '

'I can see right now you don't know our hero very well, Mr Grissom,' Myra said.

Dolan suddenly swung his foot, trying to kick her. Myra got her fanny out of the way by an inch.

'What's new here?' Bishop asked.

'Nothing but six or seven re-orders.'

'From where?'

'Drug-stores around Weston Park – '

'Right in the doctor's own back yard,' Dolan said. 'We'll send them out right away.'

'They've already gone. The kid, my apprentice, took them out.'

'You shouldn't have done that,' Dolan said. 'You should have waited. I wouldn't want to see the kid run into anything he couldn't handle – '

'I don't think he will,' Grissom said.

'Well . . .' Dolan said, walking on back to the balcony steps, going up to his office.

'I'm glad we put that deposition in the safety deposit vault, anyway,' Myra said. 'At least we know nothing can happen to it.'

'What do we do for next week?' Bishop asked.

'The first thing I'm going to do is write an editorial about the Little Theatre situation. It's not a Little Theatre at all any more. It's an exclusive stock company.'

'There's more to it than that,' Myra said from where she was sitting. 'What about it being a rendezvous for homosexuals and lesbians? What about the homes it has broken up? The people it's ruined – '

'I'll give you an argument there,' Dolan said. 'It's helped a lot of people, too. Things have been a hell of a lot better since the Major came in.'

'Oh, you want to straddle the fence where the dear Little Theatre is concerned – '

'Will you stop trying to tell me what goes on there? I helped build it. I've practically lived there for seven or eight years – '

'That's what I'm getting at. You're too close to it. You're straddling the fence. I'll write the Little Theatre editorial – '

'Well, for God's sake go on and write it then, you know so much.'

'Nobody gives a damn about that anyway,' Bishop said. 'Who's going to be our lead story? Carson?'

'Carson's little stuff – '

'Yeah? He makes fifty thousand a year on the purchase of city trucks alone.'

'Nobody gives a damn about that, either. People nowadays expect their city commissioners to be grafters, they'd probably be disappointed if they weren't. No – it's not Carson – '

'Nestor?'

'I don't know. He's a bigger crook than Carson, because he's hooked up with the underworld. He looks and talks like a farmer in spite of his Deusenberg, but he's a damn slick egg. I'm just wondering if we should start at the bottom and gradually work our way up to Mussohitler Carlisle.'

'There, of course, is something. Carlisle. If we could topple him I'd say we were in the bag for the Pulitzer award for the most meritorious public service – '

'Only they don't give it to magazines. Or should we bang away at Carlisle next? The only bad thing about that is that we're a weekly, and we've got to come out next week. If we were a monthly it would be simple. We'd have time to get our facts. I don't believe we could nail Carlisle in a week.'

'I don't either,' Bishop said. 'I think we better take Nestor. I know all there is to know about him. I can write that story without ever leaving the office – '

'That's your favourite kind of story, isn't it?' Myra said.

'Look,' Bishop said. 'This is the guy you're riding. Not me. Will you lay off?'

'Well – maybe we'd better take Nestor . . . Oh, Mr Grissom,' he called, leaning over the rail.

Grissom walked to the foot of the stairs, looking up.

'You know any advertising solicitors who might be interested in getting some business for the magazine?'

'I don't know anybody I'd recommend,' Grissom said. 'Why don't you call Jerges at the *Courier*? He might know some-body – '

'I think I will,' Dolan said, going down the steps to the telephone. 'Could we have an extension run up there? We use the telephone a lot, you know.'

'Yes, I'll order one. There's the *Courier* number on that calendar – '

Dolan dialled the *Courier* and got Jerges, explaining what he wanted. Jerges said he was pretty sure he could dig up somebody, but that he was afraid anybody he sent over would want a small weekly salary and a percentage of the business he got. Dolan said that would be all right, to send him over, and gave him Grissom's address.

'Send one of your own men, too. I want to take a half-page in the *Courier*. A personal ad. – '

Jerges said it probably would be sometime in the afternoon before he could get hold of anybody, thanked him, and hung up. Dolan went back to the foot of the stairs.

'Hey, Ed,' he called. 'You want to take a look around the news-stands with me?'

'Sure – '

'All right,' Myra said, sticking her head over the railing. 'Go ahead and overdo it – '

'You check with those women's clubs on the society calendar for next week, that's all you've got to do. You're on salary now, don't forget that – '

'We'll be back in an hour,' Bishop said.

'If an advertising solicitor comes looking for me, tell him to wait,' Dolan said.

'Better take it easy,' Myra said. 'You may be hurt worse than you think you are – '

Dolan didn't answer, walking towards the door with Bishop.

'I want to go across the street to the telephone first,' Dolan said.

'Use this one – '

'I don't want Myra to hear me. I'm going to phone McGonagill to get me another badge and a pistol. Next time I won't be so careless – '

DR HARRY CARLISLE FOUND DEAD
BODY OF SOCIETY DOCTOR DISCOVERED IN
BATHROOM
REVOLVER BESIDE HAND

the headlines read.

' "Revolver beside hand – " ' Dolan said. 'These lousy news-papers. They didn't even have nerve enough to say he committed suicide – '

' "Doctor Harry Carlisle, thirty-five-year-old surgeon and popular social leader, was found dead in the bathroom of his Weston Park mansion shortly after eleven o'clock this morn-ing," ' Bishop read. ' "A single bullet had penetrated his right temple. A revolver was found by his outstretched right hand. Doctor Carlisle was the target for a furious attack unleashed yesterday by a new Colton periodical, but none of his intimate friends would indicate whether or not he had seen it. Jack Carlisle, his brother, well known in local political circles, was too upset by the tragedy to make any statement for publication – " '

'That all one paragraph?' Dolan asked.

'No, it's several paragraphs. The way I read it made it sound like one.'

'I was going to say it was pretty bad writing . . .'

They didn't say anything for a block or two, Bishop holding the newspaper, staring at the headlines; Dolan looking straight ahead, keeping his eyes on the traffic.

. . . 'I guess we better go back to the office,' Dolan said.

'I guess we had – '

Dolan drove into the parking lot on the corner, and he and Bishop went to the office, a couple of doors away. When they entered, Grissom and Myra were in Grissom's office in front, reading the paper. They looked up and saw that Bishop also had a paper.

'Tough, hunh?' Grissom said.

'Well, I never thought he'd do that, of course,' Dolan said.

'What'd you expect him to do?' Myra asked.

'Now, for God's sake, don't tell me you anticipated this,' Dolan said roughly.

'I didn't anticipate it – no,' Myra said. 'But, by God, we should have if we'd thought about it. There was no other out for him. It was the only way to keep it from going to the Grand Jury – '

'Well, suppose we had known he was going to do it. What then? That wouldn't have stopped us from printing the story, would it?'

'I suppose not,' Myra admitted.

'Hell, I'm not sorry. I'm not going to be hypocritical. He was my enemy ever since I can remember. I hated his guts and he hated mine. Besides, he was a public enemy. The town's damn well rid of him . . . I'm not concerned about any of those things. I'm wondering what effect this will have on the magazine – '

'I didn't know the gentleman,' Grissom said, 'but if you're asking me, I think this is the best advertisement you can have. The public may or may not think this is horrible, but what about his brother's thugs attacking you last night? That was horrible, too. They might just as easily have killed you.'

'God knows they tried to,' Dolan said. 'They failed because they didn't know much about the Irish. If you ever want to kill an Irishman, never start beating on his skull.'

'I'd suggest,' Bishop said mildly, 'that we tidy the place up a bit for Jack Carlisle's visit.'

'You don't think he's coming here, do you,' Dolan said, stating a fact, not asking a question.

'I don't see how he can avoid it,' Bishop said.

'I don't think he will – not now. I'm not so sure we'll ever hear from him.'

'I'd feel better if I thought that,' Bishop said.

Two men came in, two young men.

'We're looking for Mr Dolan,' one of them said.

'I'm Dolan. What is it?'

'My name's Cook,' the man said. 'With the *Courier*. This is Mr Gage. Jerges said something about an ad. you wanted to take – '

'Yes.'

'Gage has come to talk to you about that solicitor's job. I

think you said something to Jerges about that, too. Gage used
to work for Jerges.'

'Come upstairs, gentlemen,' Dolan said, leading the way to
the balcony.

'Looks like you got a pretty bad smack,' Cook said, as they
went up the steps. 'Auto accident?'

'In a way. It's not quite as bad as it looks. Sit down – '

'Automobiles are death-traps these days,' Cook observed.

'Yes,' Dolan said. 'I want to run a half-page ad. in the
Courier tomorrow. I want it run where everybody can see it.'

'Well, anywhere in the first section is good, Mr Dolan. I'm
afraid I can't give you a specified spot at the moment on
account of most of our space being contracted for. But I'll get
you in the first section somewhere.'

'How much would that be?'

'Is it a layout or just straight copy?'

'Straight copy.'

'Two hundred dollars. If you want it in tomorrow we must
have the copy by three o'clock. Is it written yet?'

'It won't take long. I'll have it to you by three. Will you give
me a receipt?' he asked, taking out a roll of money, counting
off two hundred dollars.

Cook wrote the receipt and picked up the money.

' "This receipt in no way obligates the *Colton Courier* to
furnish the advertising space designated below," ' Dolan read
in small type, at the bottom of the slip of paper. ' "The *Courier*
reserves the right to reject any copy it deems at variance with
the policies and ideals of its tradition." '

' – Just a formality,' Cook said.

'Good thing this is a personal ad.,' Dolan said. 'From the
sound of this I might have trouble advertising the magazine – '

'You won't need much advertising for the magazine,' Cook
said. 'The *Cosmopolite* was all I heard where I went this
morning – '

'Really? Good or bad?'

'About fifty-fifty, I should say. But that doesn't matter as long as they talk about it . . . See you later, Gage. Thanks, Mr Dolan,' he said, going down the stairs.

Dolan turned to Gage.

'Ever had any experience in soliciting?'

'That's all I've done since I got out of college. Four years of it. I used to work for Jerges – '

'What happened?'

'Nothing. Business got bad, and I was laid off six months ago. I got a couple of letters of recommendation here,' he said, reaching into his pocket.

'Never mind. Of course, you know I can't pay you anything like what the *Courier* did. How much did you make there?'

'Twenty a week.'

'Twenty! Lord, it's a wonder they don't go broke. I thought you guys made sixty or seventy – '

'Some of them do, I guess. I didn't.'

'How much do you want to work for me?'

'I don't know, Mr Dolan. I'd like a little something I could count on, and then a percentage of what I sell.'

'Hey, Mike!' Bishop called from downstairs. 'We're going over and get a sandwich. You want one?'

'I want two. Bring me a couple,' Dolan said, over the railing. 'What kind?'

'Any kind. Well, Gage, do you think you can sell space in the *Cosmopolite*?'

'I can try,' Gage said, smiling.

'You don't sound very hopeful – '

'I'm not one of the Rover boys, Mr Dolan. I don't believe all that stuff I read in the magazines about high-powered salesmanship. I'll give you a run for your money, all right – '

'I believe you will, at that. Had lunch yet?'

'No, sir – '

'You don't need to be formal around here. Call me Mike. What's your name?'

'Cecil.'

'Well, Cecil, you go get some lunch and then we'll talk about
rates and things. The reason we can't talk about them now is
because I don't know a thing about them. I've never fooled
with that end before – wait a minute, we didn't agree on salary.
You got twenty a week from the *Courier*. How much do you
want from me?'

'Anything you say is all right with me.'

'How about fifteen?'

'Fine. I only hope I can bring you in some business – '

'So do I. If you don't you won't last but a week, I'll tell you
that. Here, here's five bucks on account – '

'Thank you,' Gage said, taking the money, standing up, 'I'll
be back in about half an hour . . .'

That night Dolan took five Anacin tablets in a space of forty-
five minutes, trying to stop the hammering inside his skull.

'If you'd stop pacing the floor and sit down and stop worrying about things over which you got no control, your head
would stop aching,' Myra said. 'Carlisle's dead.'

'I'm not worrying about him,' Dolan said.

'Well, what are you worrying about?'

'I'm not worrying about anything.'

'I didn't know that copy of the *New Masses* was going to
upset you,' Myra said. 'I showed you that story to prove that
this is not the only town in the country where strange things are
happening – '

'That's not what upset me,' Dolan said. 'That only made me
sore. Every day I'm finding out more to get sore about. That's
why I want to put out a bigger magazine, a national magazine,
so I can do something about these things. I think Dorothy
Sherwood had a perfect right to kill her two-year-old son. She
knew he didn't have a chance in a billion to achieve self-respect
or happiness or enough to eat – and she was right. She didn't
want that boy to grow up cursing her for having him – like I

used to do my mother. And my father. Like I still do. What goddam right did they have to bring me into the world? They couldn't take care of me, they let me learn the facts of life behind billboards and in dark alleys, goddam 'em both – '

'Mike!' Myra said sharply, getting up, going to him.

'You think this is just a wild moment I'm having? Well, lady, you're mistaken. I know exactly what I'm saying. I know exactly how Dorothy Sherwood felt! What did this country have to offer her son? What the hell has this country got to offer *any* son? A bread-line or a piece of shrapnel in the belly? Was it her fault she killed him? Why the hell didn't the jury sentence the man who brought about this condition to the chair? Hell, that would have made sense – '

'My God! The power and force you've got,' Myra said softly, staring at him. 'Michael Dolan, you're going to be a big man one of these days! You're going to be so goddam big – '

There was a knock at the door.

'Come in,' Dolan called, over his shoulder.

It was Ulysses.

'There's a man downstairs to see you,' he said.

'What about?'

'I don't know, Mister Mike. I asked him and he said it was personal.'

'What does he look like?'

'He's funny looking. Little bitty guy, with a moustache. I think he's a foreigner – '

'Didn't say what it was about?'

'No, sir. I told him I didn't think you was home. Maybe I better tell him you ain't here – '

'Bring him up, Ulysses – '

'Wait a minute, Ulysses,' Myra said. 'Look here, Mike. You know you oughtn't to be doing things like this. I wish you'd realize that we're engaged in a dangerous business.'

'Go ahead, Ulysses,' Dolan said.

Ulysses went out reluctantly, shaking his head.

'One of these days you'll wish you had listened to me,' Myra said.

Dolan smiled at her, throwing his tie on the bookcase, hanging his coat on the back of the chair. He moved to the desk and took the six-shooter (a new one, the second one McGonagill had given him, late that afternoon) out of the holster in his hip pocket and laid it on the desk, covering it with a newspaper. He arranged the chair by the desk so if he had to he could get to the gun without delay from a sitting position . . . and pretended to be very casual when Ulysses brought the stranger in.

The man obviously was a foreigner, a little shabby, and very small, a light-weight. Italian, Dolan thought. He looked worried, but Dolan wasn't sure this was genuine, having reached the point where he was suspicious of everybody.

'This here is Mister Dolan,' Ulysses said, not too graciously, walking slowly towards the door as if undecided whether or not to leave. Dolan motioned him out with his head, and the stranger waited until he was gone before he spoke.

'Mr Dolan,' he said then, 'I need your help.'

Dolan was surprised to hear the man speak precise English. To look at him you would think he would have one hell of an accent.

'Sit down,' Dolan said, watching him closely.

'My name is Bagriola,' the man said, still standing, twisting his hat, looking warily at Myra. 'I am a barber – '

'This is Miss Barnovsky. She's my secretary. Sit down – '

Bagriola nodded to Myra with a quick jerk of his head and finally sat down on the edge of the chair. Myra moved to the bookcase, a little behind him, and stood leaning on her elbow, watching him intently, hostility written all over her face. Bagriola was conscious of this, because he turned a couple of times and looked at her, a look of fear in his eyes.

'Relax, Mister Bagriola,' Dolan said. 'Nobody's going to hurt you. What did you want to see me about?'

'I'll tell you,' Bagriola said, slightly reassured, speaking directly to Dolan. 'I've been to the police and the newspapers, but nobody can help me. Today I shaved a man, and he was talking to another man about your magazine and how much courage you had to fight for what was right – '

'What do you mean, the police won't help you?'

'Twice now some men have taken me to the river bottoms and whipped me. The last time they left me tied to a tree – '

'What's that?' Dolan said. 'What men?'

'I do not know what men. They wear robes. They wear helmets. They tar and feather people.'

'Jesuschrist!' Dolan exclaimed. 'The Crusaders!'

Bagriola nodded, smiling a thin, cold smile, and stood up, taking off his coat. He slipped his tie off and started unbuttoning his shirt.

'I show you,' he said, taking off the shirt. 'Look – '

'For God's sake,' Dolan said, amazed. 'Myra, come around here and look at this – '

Bagriola's back was an artistic criss-cross of welts and cuts.

'Heavens, I can lay my finger in a couple of these valleys,' Dolan said. 'I never saw anything like this in my entire life. My God, it's a wonder you're alive – I never saw anything like this in my entire life.'

'You evidently don't know much of what goes on in this great free country of yours,' Myra said quietly.

'You ought to have those fixed by a doctor,' Dolan said to Bagriola. 'You're liable to get infection – '

'I have been to the doctor several times. Tonight I tell him to leave off the bandages, I will come show you,' Bagriola said calmly putting on his shirt again.

'Jesuschrist!' Dolan said again. 'Look here, what did the police say to you?'

'Nothing. They said unless I could identify the men they could do nothing. Of course, I couldn't do that because they wore masks and travel in a mob. Very brave men,' Bagriola said, shrugging, buttoning his shirt.

'Would you – do you want a drink or something?' Dolan asked.

'Thank you, no,' Bagriola said, smiling. 'I want only justice – '

'Well, I'll be a sonofabitch,' Dolan said to himself, still disturbed by the impact of what he had seen.

'Don't be too upset,' Bagriola said sincerely. 'I am only one. There are others – '

'Do you mean to say this sort of thing is common?'

'Very common. There are dozens and dozens. Nobody knows about them because they are not written up. That is what convinced me that somebody in the police department or the newspapers knows all about it. Why else would the facts be suppressed?'

'You speak pretty good English for a foreigner,' Myra said.

'So do you,' Bagriola said, smiling softly.

'I'm not a foreigner – '

'Neither am I. I was born in this country. Sometimes, when I am a little excited, my grammar is bad – but otherwise I speak very well. See – I am an American,' he said, holding out his coat, turning the lapel.

Through the lapel ran the red, white, and blue ribbon of the Distinguished Service Cross.

'In the Argonne. At Cunel, with the First Army,' he said.

'Yes,' Dolan said. 'You're an American, all right. If I wrote this story, people wouldn't believe it. They'd swear I invented that D.S.C. story just to make it ironic – '

'But it did happen. You can see it for yourself,' Myra said.

'Sure it happened, but I mean it's an old situation that by now nobody would believe . . . I'm sorry for interrupting, Mr Bagriola. Go ahead. Why did they whip you?'

'Immorality. They said – ' he stopped, looking self-consciously at Myra.

'Go ahead, Mr Bagriola,' Myra said.

'They said I was sleeping with my sister and my sister-in-law and my daughters – '

'How'd they happen to say that?'

'It was the natural thing, Mister Dolan. We are a very big family, and we all live in a very small house. If I had the money, I would live in a big house where everybody could have their own room – '

'But you aren't immoral, are you?'

'No, sir,' Bagriola said. 'I am not immoral. You must believe that.'

'We believe it,' Myra said. 'How did these men happen to pick on you?'

'I do not know,' Bagriola said. 'You can investigate me. I send my children to school, I am a good barber, I am religious – I pay my bills. Not all of them, but I pay some each month. I do not know how they picked me out. Neighbours, perhaps – '

'Somebody trying to get revenge on you?'

'Revenge for what? I have harmed nobody – '

'People don't need a very good reason to take men out and whip them,' Myra said. 'They just do it – '

'There are many who have been whipped. There are some who have been crippled. I know one man who was hanged by the neck – '

'What?' Dolan gasped.

'He did not die,' Bagriola said. 'They were teaching him a lesson. He will live, but he will always be paralysed. Some nerves were injured – '

'Look here – can you take me to this man?'

'Surely. Any time you say.'

'Right now. I want to go right now – '

'Just a minute, Mike. There's no use rushing this. The world's not going to end tonight.'

'Why, this is the goddamdest thing I ever heard of,' Dolan said, his thin lips white. 'I don't care what the man has done. No gang of yellow sonsabitches have got a right to string him up. Was it the same gang, Bagriola?'

'They wore black robes and black helmets. There probably are many gangs, but they all are the same organization – '

'Why, this is the goddamdest thing I ever heard of,' Dolan said, putting on his tie. 'This is a hell of a form of amusement!'

'Just the same, you're a fool to get excited about it now,' Myra said, going over to him. 'Listen, Mike. I've been around quite a bit in my time, and believe me, this is just another example of good old-fashioned Americanism. This country's full of stuff like this. My God, you can't fight the whole system single-handed. You've got to take it in stride, calmly and dis-passionately. You mustn't dissipate your energy on these things that upset you. Be rational . . . I'm assuming,' she said, turning to Bagriola, her voice cold again and the hostility in her face again, 'that what you've said is the truth?'

'It is the truth. You know it is the truth,' Bagriola said.

'I believe you, anyway,' Dolan said, putting on his coat. 'I've heard about these babies, but this is the first time I've seen a sample of their work – '

Myra walked over to the desk and lifted the newspaper off the pistol. Bagriola watched her, but not a flicker of emotion was in his pale face. Myra picked up the pistol and walked back to Dolan, putting the holster in his hip pocket, unstrapping the belt so he could run it through the slot in the holster.

'Mister Bagriola,' she said, turning to him, 'I'm inclined to believe you, too. But this is a dangerous business we're in, and we must be careful. If there is the slightest indication that you are trying to lead Dolan into a trap, he will shoot you im-mediately. Remember that.'

'It's not that bad, Bagriola,' Dolan said. 'Come on – '

'Before you leave,' Myra said to Bagriola, 'would you mind giving me the address of your barber shop and your home?'

'My barber shop is at ten-thirty-eight North Las Cruces. My house is next door, ten forty.'

'Thank you,' Myra said, writing them down. 'Mike, if I don't hear from you in two hours, I shall get McGonagill and come to this address. You'd better see that he gets home safely, Mister Bagriola.'

'Now, will you please not telephone Ed and bother him?' Dolan said to her. 'His kid is still sick, and anyway he'll probably have to work nights from now on. Please don't bother him.'

'That's exactly what I intend to do,' Myra said firmly. 'I am going to phone him, I am going downstairs and get Ernst's Luger, and I am going to stand by. I don't like the looks of this a bit. I think you're a goddam obstinate fool, that's what I think – '

'Come on, Bagriola,' Dolan said, starting out. 'She loves to be dramatic . . .'

An hour and a half later Dolan returned to his apartment and found Myra and Bishop sitting there waiting for him.

'I'm sorry she got you down here, Ed,' he said. 'You see, wise guy,' he said savagely to her. 'I'm back. Nothing happened. I knew damn well nothing happened.'

'It's a good thing,' Myra said. 'I was on the level about getting McGonagill and coming after you – '

'I suppose she's told you about Bagriola?'

'From A to Z. Did you see the gentleman who was paralysed by them?'

'Yes, I saw him. Bagriola also took me to a Negro who had been severely whipped. This is what these Crusaders've been up to. I tried to get Thomas to print this story when I was on the paper. All this might have been prevented.'

'This Bagriola guy is a sort of ambassador for the oppressed, I take it – '

'This may be very funny to you, Ed – but I wish you could have seen what I saw. It was awful.'

'I don't doubt it,' Bishop said. 'Many things are awful. You went through the war. That was awful. Everything is awful. But why do you get so much steam up about this particular thing? Why don't you take it in your stride?'

'I get it,' Dolan said. 'That last remark tells me all I want to know. She thinks everything I do is wrong – '

'She doesn't think so at all,' Bishop said.

'She's always snapping and barking and fighting – '

'Well, you silly bastard, that's because she's in love with you.'

'Ed!' Myra exclaimed.

'Certainly it is,' Bishop went on calmly. 'It's time somebody told this silly bastard that – '

'Just the same,' Dolan said finally, 'I know what I saw tonight, and I know that nothing in the world can prevent me from doing something about it. Not, by God, if I get killed doing it!'

'That's fine,' Bishop said. 'Nobody's trying to keep you from doing anything about it. We're trying to help you. We want to do something about it, too. But you can't go slam-bang into things like this with nothing but your outraged sense of justice to help you. You can't clean up the whole world overnight.'

'No? Well, I'm going to slam-bang into this – '

'What about Nestor? What about Carlisle? I thought we were going to get them first?'

'There's plenty of time for them later. This thing I've run across tonight is big. It's the goddamdest biggest thing you ever heard of. Look. You remember the Ku Klux Klan, don't you?'

'Very, very well. Sit down. Take off your hat.'

'Well,' Dolan went on, standing up, keeping his hat on, 'I don't know whether this is the Klan or not. These fellows wear black outfits and call themselves The Crusaders. At any rate, they were inspired by the Klan. God knows how many members they've got – thousands. It's all very secret and very mysterious – and not a word about them has been in the newspapers. They take people out at night and whip them and tar and feather them, just like the Kian used to do – make people kiss the flag and all that stuff – for God's sake, they even made poor Bagriola kiss the flag after they'd whipped him, and he's got a war decoration and is a better American than any one of those sonsabitches. And that poor guy Trowbridge, lying there in that bed, not able to move – I can't help it if I'm hopped up about this. It makes my blood boil – '

'All right,' Bishop said. 'I listened patiently to you, and now you listen to me. I'm going to tell you something I've intended telling you for a long time. I think it's swell that you're steamed up about this. I honestly do. So does Myra. But what goes on in Colton goes on in every town in the United States. The graft and corruption, the bigotry, the fake patriotism – all that – goes on everywhere. Colton is typical and symbolic of the whole rotten mess. Suppose you end this Klan or Crusader business, whatever it is. Suppose you end it in Colton – '

'I'm going to end it, all right – '

'Wait a minute, goddam it, stop interrupting. Suppose you do smash this thing in Colton? What about the rest of the country? You can't do any permanent good until you get at the heart of it. You might end it here, yes – and next month it'll pop right up again. You see what I'm driving at?'

'Frankly, I don't. I haven't the faintest idea what you're driving at – '

'I'll put it another way. Did you ever hear of a man named Marx?'

'Sure, I've heard of Marx and Engels and Lenin. So what?'

'Know anything about them?'

'No, not much. What the hell has that got to do with this?' Bishop turned to Myra.

'Isn't this marvellous?' he said. 'Would you believe it?'

'Hardly – '

'For God's sake, what is this?' Dolan said, sore.

'The reason I asked you was because you ought to study them,' Bishop said. 'They felt the same way you do about things. They anticipated you by a good many years.'

'I still don't see – '

'I hardly know how to make you see,' Bishop said. 'You

need discipline. You need organization. Without them you won't
get to first base. Without them you're just a zealous worker.
You know what Communism is, don't you?'

'Vaguely I do, yes.'

'You're always kidding me about being a goddam
Communist – '

'I didn't mean anything personal, Ed – you know that. It was
just an expression.'

'Don't apologize,' Bishop said. 'I'm proud of it. But you're
right when you said it was just an expression. That's what it is
to most people. Why, for God's sake, you're more of a
Communist than I am – '

'You're crazy,' Dolan said. 'I'm not a Communist – '

'You're a Communist, only you don't know it. You hate the
way they run the city and you hate the way they run the Little
Theatre – you hate lousy advertising on the radio, you hate
preachers because they whine and beg for converts, you hate
the whole system. Why, goddam it, you've told me so a hundred
times – '

'Look,' Dolan said, taking off his hat. 'This argument could
go on all night. Maybe I am a Communist. If I am, I don't
know it. But I do hate all the things you say I hate, and a lot
more you didn't mention, like the Father's Day racket and the
Mother's Day racket – but most of all I hate these bastards who
put on black robes and helmets and take people down in the
river bottom and whip hell out of 'em and perform operations
on 'em and make 'em kiss the flag. Maybe I do need discipline
and organization, and maybe later on I'll get somebody to teach
them to me. But I haven't got time to stop for that now. All that
matters now is busting up those Crusaders, and I'm going to
do that if it's the last thing I ever do – '

'You'll get rich doing that,' Bishop said, with a trace of
sarcasm.

'Well, there's no pockets in a shroud,' Dolan said. 'I've never
felt like this before. A few things've annoyed me, and in a half-

hearted way I've wanted to do something about them. But I distributed my energy – and the women got most of it. There's nothing amazing about that; everybody knows I was a pushover for a good-looking girl. But there's nothing amazing in me waking up all of a sudden either. A man goes to bed tonight a fool and tomorrow morning he wakes up a wise man. He can't explain what's happened in between; all he knows is it's *happened*. That's the way it was with me. I don't know yet what I'm going to do, I haven't the faintest idea where I'm going to start – but I do know I'm going to do it.

'I don't give a damn for your Communism and your rules and regulations. As long as men come to me, as Tim Adamson did, asking me to help him at the Little Theatre, and as Bagriola did tonight, I know I'm on the right track. Maybe you can fight things like these with rules and manuals and scientific tactics, but I don't think so. Now, there'll be no more arguments, no more left-handed advice – from right now on, you two will do what I want done the way I want it done or it's hail and farewell. I mean it, by God. First thing in the morning we start after these so-called Crusaders, and nothing else matters – and right now is the time to make up your minds. Is it yes or no?'

Bishop looked at Myra, biting his lip. There was nothing in her face that he could read.

'Well, Myra,' he said finally, 'it's the wrong way to do it, but it looks like we'll have to string along with him.'

'Yes,' Myra said huskily.

'All right,' Bishop said to him. 'You're dead wrong, but you're a thick-headed Mick with a one-way mind, and Jesus Christ Himself couldn't convince you in a million years. But we'll stick because we both love you. If by some miracle we get out of this, maybe I'll have time to show you where you're all wet.'

'That's fine . . .' Dolan said. 'Now, will you please get the hell out of here and let me go to bed? My goddam head is about to pop off my shoulders – '

Bishop and Myra got up. Bishop picked his hat off the desk and went out slowly without even saying good night. Myra walked over to her coat on the bookcase and took a lot of time putting it on. Nothing was said. You could hear the ticking of the small alarm clock on the night table . . . At the door, Myra turned and looked at Dolan, still not saying anything, still not smiling – just looking. Then she went out. In a minute he heard her following Bishop down the stairs.

It did not occur to him until he got in bed that this was the only time since he had known her that she had gone to her own room without first having an argument about spending the night with him. He didn't quite know what to make of this.

3

HE was in the downstairs bathroom the following morning (the upstairs one was still haywire; Mrs Ratcliff, the owner, still refusing to budge an inch), under the shower, washing, dabbing at his body, careful not to get the bandages on his head wet, when the door suddenly burst open. Dolan paid no attention, thinking it was one of the boys, until Elbert, who was shaving, uttered a shrill squeal of surprise.

Dolan parted the curtains and looked out. Just inside the door stood Roy Menefee, his face flushed and excited, a pistol in his hand.

'Come out of there,' he said to Dolan.

'I'm coming,' Dolan said, shutting off the water, throwing the curtains back, but still standing in the tub. 'What's the matter?'

'Where's April?'

'I don't know where April is. Why ask me?'

'Stop lying, Dolan – and tell me.'

'I am telling you. I don't know where she is. I haven't seen her in several days.'

'I'm going to kill you, you lying sonofabitch – '

It was almost funny to Dolan; Menefee, meek Menefee, standing there with a gun; Elbert watching him in horror, his arm still crooked, holding the razor against his face, afraid to move it. It was almost funny...

'Wait a minute, Roy,' Dolan said, not daring to move a muscle except to talk with. 'I don't know where your wife is. I've been busy as hell for a week and I haven't seen her. I haven't even heard from her. Have I, Elbert? Has she been here?'

'No – ' Elbert managed to say.

'That's the God's truth, Roy – '

'Where else would she spend the night?' Menefee asked. 'She hasn't been home all night – '

'I don't know where she was, but she wasn't here. You can look upstairs at my bed. She didn't stay here. Anybody in the house'll tell you that. Put that gun away, Roy – you're absolutely mistaken this time.'

Menefee hesitated, but lowered the pistol, finally putting it in his pocket. He was under a great emotional strain. His face was still flushed, and he was blinking his eyes rapidly. Dolan knew that was to keep back the tears. He got out of the tub, wrapping a towel around him.

'Elbert,' he said, 'leave us alone a few minutes – '

Elbert nodded, walking out, still holding the razor.

'Here, Roy,' Dolan said, letting down the lid of the toilet seat. 'Sit down – '

Menefee walked over and sat down, his lips twitching.

'What made you think April was here?' Dolan asked.

'She's somewhere. I knew she used to have a crush on you – it's that Little Theatre that's done it. I've been trying to get her away from there for months.'

'Maybe the Little Theatre's not wholly to blame,' Dolan said, wiping his legs on the towel. 'Maybe April's a little to blame. Not that there's any harm in April – she's just naturally flirtatious. You know that – '

'I know she's slept with everybody in town. I know that. I found that out after I had married her.'

'Well – '

'Don't try to defend her, Dolan. You've slept with her yourself. I know that, too.'

'I haven't slept with her since she's been married – '

'You've had affairs with her since she's been engaged. What's the difference?'

'Hell of a lot. Look, Roy. You can't afford to be quick-tempered about this. You're liable to get into trouble with that gun – '

'I'm going to kill the man she was with last night,' he said calmly.

'And what? You'll be disgraced for life, maybe hanged. You're no bum; you're important people. No woman's worth going through that for.'

'I'm not thinking of April. I'm thinking of something else.'

'Pride?'

'Perhaps – well, I'm going. I'm going to the Little Theatre,' he said, getting up. 'If you're not the man, then he's around the Little Theatre. I'll find him,' he said, walking out.

Dolan watched him go, then picked up his robe and shoved his feet into the red slippers. He went out into the living-room and watched through the windows as Menefee got into his Packard coupé and drove off, fast. Then he went to the telephone and called the Little Theatre. They answered backstage and he asked to be transferred to the office. He waited a moment or two, and David answered.

'This is Mike Dolan, Dave,' he said. 'Okay... You get it?... Thanks for lending it to me. I left the cheque with Arlene, I wanted to pay you while I had it. Listen, Dave. Roy Menefee was just here with blood in his eye. He's looking for April and he's got a gun. He's on the way over there, and I thought you'd better tip the guys off to keep quiet about that electrician or else tell the guy to beat it... I don't know, she didn't go home last night. Menefee's desperate... Okay. Sure, I'll see you one of these days...'

He hung up and Elbert came up to him. The shaving soap had dried on his face.

'That was a narrow escape, wasn't it?' he said.

'Yes – '

'I was plenty scared for a minute, all right. God, a fellow never knows when some goofy guy is going to bump him off...'

Dolan walked off towards the stairs, not replying. His head was beginning to throb again.

'Well – I hardly knew you in your bandage,' Myra said cheerfully, as he walked into the office. 'What did the doctor say?'

'It's healing good. Couple of days and I'll be all right.'

'Hello, Dolan,' Grissom said.

'Hello – '

'Look,' Myra said, showing him a list of names. 'Nine people already have called up for annual subscriptions. Volunteers.'

'I told you that Carlisle thing was good advertising,' Grissom said.

'And Thomas called a couple of times. Said he wanted you to be in his office at noon. Very important. Big meeting or something – '

'What kind of a meeting?'

'He didn't say. Impressed on me the necessity for you to be there. Said it would be to your great advantage.'

'I haven't got time to fool with him,' Dolan said, frowning. 'What the hell can he want?'

'It won't do any harm to go see – '

'Maybe I will,' Dolan said, sitting down at the telephone, dialling the courthouse. He asked for the sheriff's office and finally got McGonagill on the telephone. Dolan said it was important that he see him at once. McGonagill said he'd better make it that night, because it wouldn't be wise for Dolan to come to the courthouse.

'Can't you run over here a minute?' Dolan asked. 'I wouldn't bother you, Bud – but this is pretty hot. I'll only keep you five minutes – '

McGonagill said all right, he'd come over.

'It's on Sixth Avenue, just off Terminal. Grissom's Publishing Company . . . Thanks, Bud.'

He replaced the receiver and stood up.

'I think it's fine about the subscriptions, Myra,' he said. 'Hello, Ed – how's the kid today?'

'Better, thanks – '

'Good. I'm going over and get a cup of coffee. I'll be back before McGonagill gets here – '

He went to the drug-store and was gratified to see they had a dozen or more *Cosmopolites* in the rack. He sat down at the fountain and ordered a cup of coffee. He drank it slowly and then went across the street to the office. Myra said she had two more subscriptions . . .

Ten minutes later McGonagill walked in the front door and spoke to Grissom. Grissom pointed upstairs and went over and sat down with Myra, talking to her.

'Sorry to trouble you, Bud,' Dolan said.

'That's okay, Mike,' McGonagill said, a little gruffly. 'How're you, Ed – '

'All right, Bud,' Bishop said. 'Sit down.'

'I ran into something last night I thought you might help me with,' Dolan said. 'You and Chief Emmett are the only men in town who can help me. I wanted to speak to you first.'

'Okay. What is it?'

'Did you ever hear of The Crusaders?'

'Why – no. Who are they?'

'You have heard of them, Bud,' Dolan said quietly. 'When you narrow your eyes and look over the tip of your nose you give yourself away. Who are they?'

'For God's sake, Mike. Is that all you wanted to ask me?'

'All! Don't you think that's plenty?'

'I don't know. I never heard of The Crusaders – '

'It's like the Epworth League – only different,' Bishop said, a trifle sarcastic.

'Bud,' Dolan said, leaning over, 'let's cut out the stalling. You know goddam well who they are. Hell, you can't help but know – '

'When did you find out about them?'

'Last night. This morning.'

'Well, if you just found out this morning, don't you think it's possible I might not have found out yet?'

'No, it's not. I met a man last night named Trowbridge. His wife said she'd talked to you personally about these Crusaders.'

'Trowbridge? I don't remember anybody named Trowbridge.'

'You ought to. She's the wife of the guy they strung up – the guy they paralysed – '

'I still don't remember,' McGonagill said, shaking his head. 'Maybe I met her and don't remember her. I meet a hell of a lot of people, you know – '

'Oh hell, Bud. I know you know who these Crusaders are – you know damn well I do. Why are you so jittery about talking?'

'You got me wrong, Mike. I'm not jittery. I'd talk if I knew anything – '

'You're going to talk to me – you can bet your life you're going to – '

'Now, hold on there, Mike,' McGonagill said, getting up, a dark look on his face. 'This has gone far enough. You're a good guy and I like you, but I'm goddamed if I'm going to let you shove me around – '

'I'm going to shove you around plenty if you don't tell me something. I'm not impressed by either the look on your face or the notches on your gun. You're in no position to get ritzy with me. I know a lot of people who're waiting to get at your throat. If you don't talk to me, I'll throw you to the wolves so goddam fast it'll make your head swim. I mean it.'

McGonagill looked around the balcony and then over the railing.

'Let's go downstairs,' he said, after a pause.

'That's more like it,' Dolan said, leading the way.

At the foot of the stairs Dolan turned and went back by the washroom.

'I can't tell you much, because I don't know much,'

McGonagill said. 'But just between me and you, I hope you can do something. Another month and they'll be running the country. They're worse than the Ku Klux.'

'They can't be worse. Are you a member?'

'Hell, no. They never asked me.'

'You know anybody who is a member?'

'I'm pretty sure Sam Wren is. He's one of my deputies. I think Crenshaw is, too. I think he's one of the leaders.'

'Marvin Crenshaw – '

'Yeah – '

'Why, he's vice-president of the Colton National. He's one of the biggest guys in town. President of the Chamber of Commerce – '

'Just the same, Marvin Crenshaw is one of the leaders. You understand, none of this I'm telling you is personal knowledge. It's what I've heard around – '

'I understand. Don't worry, this is one time I'm not going off half-cocked. But, no matter what happens, I'll be careful and not involve you.'

'Yes, for God's sake, be careful. Those other guys you were after is kindergarten stuff compared with this. That's why I've never paid any attention to the complaints. I can't afford to – '

'There's just one other thing, Bud – and if you do this I'll never ask another favour. I want you to find out from Wren when and where the next meeting will be held – '

'I can't do that, Mike. This is a hell of a secret organization. I might make Sam suspicious – '

'I'll leave that to you. You've had enough experience to handle it. After all, you're his superior officer.'

'Well, you'd never know it. Lately he's been pretty snotty. Bullying around – '

'He's lost his respect for you. He's probably after your job.'

'I know he is – '

'All right – so much more the reason you should help me.

You find out when and where they meet and I'll smash 'em. I promise you that.'

'Okay. I'll do my best. But for God's sake – '

'I'll protect you, Bud. Thanks for coming over.'

McGonagill nodded and went out. Dolan went upstairs.

'What the hell was he stalling for?' Bishop said.

'I don't think he knows a lot – '

'The hell he doesn't. He's one of 'em himself – '

'I don't believe it. He's promised to help all he can – '

'Yeah? He's yellow. He's got a lot of guts when it comes to shooting people, but he's yellow when it comes to an issue like this. He's so goddam yellow he won't fight for his own family – '

'I'm going over to see Thomas,' Dolan said, cutting him off, going downstairs.

'. . . You want to have lunch with us?' Myra asked.

'I don't know how long I'll be,' Dolan said. 'I'm going to see Thomas – '

Dolan went into Thomas's office, looked for him, and the secretary said he was in the conference room on the second floor and had left word that if Dolan showed up he was to come right down. Dolan went outside into the city room, pausing before the old letter-box a moment under a wave of faint nostalgia. He was conscious of a terrific clatter in his ears as he turned around; it was the same place – typewriters going, teletype going, people moving and scraping, and then he realized that these were the same old sounds, too, only they seemed louder now because he had been away for weeks . . .

The faint nostalgia he had felt a moment ago was gone now, and he stood there, hoping it would return, hoping it would come back in a devastating fashion, a terrific flood of home-sickness that would bury his stomach and heart and roll out his ears and make him wish he were back working here. He had always heard Once a Reporter, Always a Reporter, and a lot of

other traditional saws about The Smell of Ink in Your Nostrils
and The Quiver of Excitement When News is Breaking, etc.;
but he knew now this was a lot of nonsense. He was disappointed to discover this. It was one of the first things he had
ever learned, but now he knew that was a lot of crap, too.
Several reporters were looking at him, and a couple of the old
men in the copy slot, but none of them spoke or even indicated
his presence by so much as a nod of the head or a wave of the
hand.

Dolan turned out of the office and went down the steps to
the conference room, knowing in his heart that he was going
over a bridge he never again would cross . . . and walking
towards the library he was thinking

> glad
> sad
> glad
> sad
> glad
> sad glad sad glad sad glad sad glad sad glad sad glad
> sad glad sad gladsadgladsadgladsadgladsadglad
> sadgladsadgladsad

without truly finding out which he was.

He opened the conference-room door and went inside.

The six men sitting around the table stopped talking and
looked up. Dolan knew them all: Thomas, at the head of the
table; Mastenbaum, publisher of the *Index*, the big morning
paper; Havetry, publisher of the *Courier*; Riddle, secretary-
treasurer of the *Star*, the smallest afternoon paper; Sandrich,
his managing editor; and Barriger, city editor of the *Times-
Gazette*.

'Come in, Dolan,' Thomas said, getting up, indicating a
leather chair beside him at the head of the table. 'We're glad
you're here. You know these gentlemen, don't you – ?'

'Yes. How do you do?' Dolan said, nodding.

'Sit down. What's the matter with your head?'

'Oh – an accident – '

'Too bad. Sit down,' Thomas said again. 'Shall I tell Dolan why we're here?' he asked the assembly.

A couple of the men grunted.

'Dolan,' Thomas said, 'this is rather an unusual procedure, this meeting. All the newspapers are represented here for a common cause. I may as well inform you now that we are determined to fight for our rights. By that I mean we are not going to have our circulations jeopardized. We have asked you to come here to make you a proposition – '

Dolan said nothing, waiting for him to go on.

'We have agreed to give you twenty-five hundred dollars each – a total of ten thousand dollars – and arrange to get you a job with any newspaper you suggest, in any metropolitan city, provided that city is at least one thousand miles from Colton, if you will give up this magazine and sign an agreement never to start another one here.'

'Why are you making me this offer?' Dolan asked.

'We'll be frank with you. There are a great many subjects you can handle in your magazine which the newspaper cannot, because of innumerable ramifications, touch or even hint at. Those subjects make good reading, because they are destructive – and you have a concrete example in the suicide of Doctor Harry Carlisle – '

'Was it suicide?'

'Of course it was!'

'I didn't know. I had to figure it out from reading the newspapers. None of them said it was suicide. They said he was found dead with a pistol beside him.'

'Don't quibble, Dolan. This is not a debate on how or what the newspapers shall say or the style in which they say it. The fact remains that the *Cosmopolite* is responsible for Carlisle's death, and this is bound to impress a certain class of people, morons probably, with the fearlessness of the magazine.'

'Gentlemen,' Dolan said smiling, speaking to the entire group, 'do you realize this is an admission of defeat? Don't you know you're admitting that any paper or periodical which even gets around the edges of the truth in this town is bound to succeed?'

'That is all beside the point,' Thomas said. 'We have made you a very generous offer. Of course, if you want to be recalcitrant, there are other ways to handle the situation – '

'I suppose by that remark you mean unless I take this money and go to New York, I'll get what Whittelsey got. He started a tabloid here and lasted about three months – and then he was strong-armed into leaving. Is that what you mean?'

'Oh, don't be stupid about it,' Thomas said irritably. 'Ten thousand dollars and a job anywhere you want. That will pay all your bills and leave you plenty besides – '

'I've got plenty,' Dolan said. 'As a matter of fact, I took an ad. in the *Courier* this afternoon along those lines – '

'Then you refuse?'

'Yes – but I'm not sorry I came. You may not think so, but this is a major triumph for me – '

'All right,' Thomas said. 'Get all you can out of it, because it'll probably be your last – '

'Maybe,' Mastenbaum said, from across the table, 'we might raise the ante a little – '

'Never mind, Mister Mastenbaum,' Thomas said. 'I know him better than you do. It's hopeless – '

They stared at him, and Dolan finally realized they had nothing else to say to him, that they had assembled only in an effort to impress him with a solid front of awesome importance.

'Good-bye, gentlemen,' he said, getting up, going out.

He walked to the end of the corridor and waited for the elevator.

A man came charging down the steps behind the latticed elevator cage. It was Bassett, one of the copy readers. He tore around the corner and ran down the corridor. Half-way to the

conference room he met Thomas and the other executives and
had an animated and brief conversation. Thomas and Barriger
started running out, going up the stairs two at a time. Bassett
jumped in the elevator with Dolan, going down. He was very
excited.

'What's the matter?' Dolan asked.

'I got to tell the circulation department to round up some
hustlers. We're going extra – '

'On what?'

'Big Weston Park murder. Roy Menefee just killed his wife
and another guy – '

The elevator stopped at the ground floor. Bassett swung out
and rushed through a door into the business office.

' – What's the matter with your head, Mister Mike?' asked
Edward, the ancient Negro elevator operator.

He got no answer. He shook his head, puzzled, watching
Dolan walk on through the big doors into the street . . .

There were only two things in the paper that Dolan looked at
that afternoon.

One was the page-one story in hand-set headlines:

WESTON PARK SCION
SLAYS DÉBUTANTE WIFE AND MAN

ROY MENEFEE KILLS COUGHLIN MENEFEE

AND EMIL VIDEO, LITTLE THEATRE ELECTRICIAN,

IN DOWNTOWN ROOMING-HOUSE

He did not read the story.

The other thing he looked at was the personal advertisement
he had bought and which was on the lower half of page ten. It
was set in enormous type, in a wide box:

TO MY CREDITORS: LARGE AND

SMALL

I have lately come into a considerable sum of money. It is my desire to pay off all my obligations, regardless of how long they have been outstanding. Therefore, if I owe you any money at all, for merchandise or for personal loans, come to 812 Sixth Avenue tomorrow afternoon at 3 o'clock and you will be paid in full.

MICHAEL DOLAN
(former sports editor,
Times-Gazette),
Now Publisher and Editor,
the *Cosmopolite*,
The Truth, the Whole
Truth, and Nothing
but the Truth.

Dolan had been badgered by creditors for so many years that he had dreamed of the day when he would be able to run this ad. It had been an obsession with him.

But now the kick was gone.

He left early that afternoon and drove to the beach. He was gone for hours, but he had no recollection of anything definite he had done or seen. He couldn't remember whether or not he had had dinner. When he got home, Bishop and Myra were waiting for him.

'We've been waiting hours,' Myra said.

'I'm sorry. I went for a ride.'

'Apparently it doesn't do any good to tell you that you shouldn't be doing things like that,' Bishop said. 'So I guess I'll save my breath. However, we would like to know what Thomas wanted – '

Dolan told them. Bishop was not surprised.

'That's a tribute,' he said. 'It's without precedent.'

'It's a swell situation for a story,' Myra said.

'We haven't hurt their circulation any yet,' Dolan said, 'but

I do believe they realize we are a definite threat.'

'No,' Bishop said, shaking his head, 'it's not their circulation they're afraid of – it's their prestige. That's what's eating them. They don't want their readers to know they're being cheated – '

'Maybe you're right. . . That was a hell of a thing Menefee pulled, wasn't it?'

'Yeah – '

'I wonder why he shot April? He knew she was that way. He told me so this morning – '

'Did you see him this morning?' Myra asked.

'He came here looking for her. With a gun. He thought she'd spent the night here.'

'You didn't say anything about that – '

'I forgot it. Hell,' he exclaimed, turning to her, 'do I have to tell you everything that happens? I forgot it.'

'All right, all right, you forgot it,' Myra said.

'. . . Wasn't that a hell of a thing he did?' Dolan said again, to nobody. 'The guy had everything in the world – position, money, popularity – and one wild impulse and the whole thing is shattered. I guess old man Coughlin is sorry now he didn't let April marry me – '

'You're just as well off,' Bishop said. 'That never would have worked out.'

'Just the same, I'd have liked to have a crack at it – '

'For God's sake, sit down and stop that pacing!' Myra said . . .

There was a knock at the door.

'Come in,' Dolan said.

It was Elbert and Ernst.

'Excuse us,' Elbert said. 'We didn't know you had company – '

'Come in, come in,' Dolan said.

'We were just wondering if you'd made up your mind what to do about the house,' Elbert said.

'What house? This one? Do about what?'

'We've got to move. Didn't Ulysses tell you?'

'I haven't seen Ulysses,' Dolan said.

'We saw him,' Myra said. 'He told us. I forgot to tell you. You're moving – '

'Why?'

'Mrs Ratcliff's sold this property, and we've got to get out right away,' Elbert said. 'Tomorrow. They're going to put up an oil station.'

'They want to start tearing the house down right away,' Ernst said.

'They can start tonight if they want to,' Dolan said. 'I haven't got much stuff to move.'

'Tommy and Ulysses and I went out this afternoon looking for a new place,' Elbert said. 'I think we've found one over on Sycamore Street – just about the same layout as this one. If you like it we can move your stuff for you. You won't have to fool with that – '

'I don't care about seeing it,' Dolan said. 'If it's all right with the rest of you, it's all right with me.'

'Swell. Then you are going to stay with us?'

'Certainly, I'm going to stay with you.'

'Swell. That's what we wanted to find out. We'll talk to you later – in the morning. There're still a few little details to be discussed – '

'All right – '

They nodded and went out, closing the door.

' – Details,' Myra said shortly. 'You know what that means, don't you? It means dough for the rent. Why don't you get wise to yourself and kick these parasites out in the gutter where they belong?'

'It's not a bad gutter, at that,' Dolan said, slightly annoyed by the bite in her tone. 'I came out of it – why are you so jealous of these fellows? They've got a hell of a lot of talent. Geniuses, maybe.'

'Oh, for God's sake,' Myra said, curling her lips. 'They're four-flushers. They're not even good four-flushers. They're playing at being Bohemians. Don't you know that stuff's dated now?'

'Will you lay off?' Bishop growled . . . 'Mike, that Gage kid you put to soliciting looks like he might turn out pretty good. He hooked a couple of nice ads. this afternoon.'

'Good. Look, do you think I'll be involved in this thing? I mean, do you think I'll have to go to court?'

'I don't know – '

'Hell, that'd be awful – '

There was another knock at the door.

'Come in,' Dolan said.

The door opened. It was Ulysses, but he did not come in. He motioned for Dolan to come outside. He went out into the living-room, closing the door behind him.

'There's a man downstairs in a car wants to see you,' Ulysses said.

'What man? Who is he?'

'He said to tell you it was Bud and you'd know – '

'Oh – sure. I'll go right down,' he said, starting away.

He heard the door open behind him.

'Mike!' Bishop called. 'Where're you going?'

Dolan turned and went back to him.

'I'm going downstairs to see Bud McGonagill a moment. Do you mind?'

'How do you know it's McGonagill?'

'Listen. For God's sake, will you stay here with Myra and let me alone for a minute?'

He went downstairs. Bud McGonagill was sitting in a county car in the darkness.

'I didn't want to come upstairs,' McGonagill said. 'From now on we've got to be careful. I found out where The Crusaders are meeting tonight – '

'Tonight?'

'Yeah, there's a party of some kind. You know where the old airport is? Up by the reservoir?'

'I know. On the other side of the river bottoms – '

'That's right. They're meeting there at midnight. Here,' he said, lifting a bundle wrapped in newspaper. 'Use this – '

'What is it?'

'The uniform. You couldn't get close to it without putting it on.'

'Where'd you get a uniform? I thought you said you weren't a member?'

'I'm not. Belongs to Sam Wren. I assigned him to take a couple of prisoners to the pen this afternoon. Then I used my pass key and got this out of his locker. Get it back to me first thing in the morning, and I'll have it back in there and he'll never know the difference.'

'Thanks, Bud,' Dolan said, taking the bundle. 'Thanks a lot. I'll take care of it and see that you get it back in the morning.'

'Never mind that. I'll drop by here and pick it up on my way down. I guess I can take a chance for that – '

'Thanks, Bud. This is swell.'

'Forget it,' McGonagill said, starting the motor. 'Just see that nothing happens to it. And, Mike – better take your gun along. I think you can get away with this – but better take it anyway – '

'Thanks, Bud – '

When McGonagill had driven off, Dolan went back upstairs with the bundle.

'What's that?' Bishop asked.

'A new suit,' Dolan said, starting to unwrap it.

'When did McGonagill go in the tailoring business?' Myra asked.

'Damn good thing for us that he did,' Dolan said, opening the bundle.

He lifted up a black robe and a black helmet.

'For God's sake!' Bishop said.

'What is this?' Myra said.

Dolan held up the robe. It was very long, and voluminous, big enough to cover two men. On the front of it was an old English C in white, with a red arrow through it. The helmet was simply a piece of black cloth sewed together with holes stitched in for the eyes, nose, and mouth. It had a smaller old English C on the forehead.

'Know now?' Dolan said.

'It's the Crusaders' uniform. What the hell are you going to do with it?'

'Wear it. I'm going to their meeting tonight – '

'Why, you goddam fool,' Myra said.

'Look at this cheap material,' Dolan said, showing the robe. 'Don't you know somebody got rich selling these things?'

' – So McGonagill did know something,' Bishop said.

'He's on our side,' Dolan said. 'He's helping me – '

'He's helping you get killed – '

Bishop and Myra looked at each other. They knew instinctively what each was thinking: that there was no use trying to talk to him about going to the meeting, that he was a goddamed hard-headed Mick with a one-way mind, and that he was going to do this in spite of hell and high-water . . . and Dolan knew what they were thinking, too.

'It's no use,' he said. 'May as well spare yourself the effort. I told you I was after these bastards, and I meant it. I'm going – '

'Then all we can do,' Bishop said, 'is to hope that you get out of it alive – '

'I guess it is,' Dolan said . . .

He did not get into much traffic until he was about a mile across the river bottoms, going up the old reservoir road. It was a narrow road and very bumpy, covered only with a layer of macadam. It was not used any more by motor traffic, once upon a time it had been the main artery north, but that was in the old days before the fine highways and fast cars. Now it was used only by a few farmers who lived far back in the hills. Farmers and Crusaders.

Dolan drove along very carefully, hugging the right side of the road, leaving plenty of room on the left and plenty of room in front. He did not want to have an accident here. Even so small a thing as a crumpled fender might be disastrous. He did not want to talk to anybody or even see anybody. That was why he had the collar of his trench coat pulled up behind his hat, and his hat well down over his eyes. There was not one chance in a thousand that he would be recognized thus by somebody driving along, but he couldn't risk even that. Presently his progress became slower, and he could see the cars choking up far in front of him. It was like the traffic in the Arroyo Seco after a Rose Bowl game. He nursed his car along, trying to keep his mind on this so he would not have to think about what he was going to do when he got where he was going, wherever that was. He didn't even know that.

But it was a difficult job to keep from thinking about this, because it was mysterious and dangerous. His heart was pumping very fast. He was having a little trouble breathing. He was excited. He was glad there were hundreds of cars behind him. He couldn't turn around and go back now even if he wanted to. I don't want to, he thought, but I am glad they are there, because if I did want to I couldn't.

Slower and slower the cars moved ahead, and presently he had to stop hugging the right side of the road so tightly, because he was beginning to pass parked automobiles. He wondered, suddenly (and was a little panicky because he hadn't thought about it before) if they would ask him for a card. That was probably the reason the automobiles were slowing down so much; there was somebody up ahead stopping the cars, asking to see membership cards. The more he thought about this the more convinced he was that this was what was happening. He wished now he'd thought to ask McGonagill for Wren's card.

But that wouldn't have helped much; hell, the man who was asking for cards would certainly know he wasn't Sam Wren. And what if McGonagill had double-crossed him and told them he was coming. Look out for a guy named Mike Dolan. Six-footer, black hair, driving an old Chevrolet roadster. He's out to expose you. Look out for him. Be sure and stop all cars. What if McGonagill had crossed him up? Oh, Bud wouldn't do a thing like that, his conscious mind said. No! his subconscious mind said. Better not trust him too far. But, hell, his conscious mind said he's my friend. I helped him get elected, I helped his kid get a scholarship in college, I started all that All-American publicity myself. I even wrote letters to Christy Walsh and Grant Rice and Corum and those guys. Bud's honest. He's on the level. Better not trust him too far, his subconscious mind said. Better park the car somewhere and get your bearings.

'That's a good idea,' Dolan said to himself.

He passed up a couple of parking places, trying to make up his mind to stop, and by the time he had decided he had passed them. In a moment he found a hole and twisted in and parked the car, turning out the lights before he cut off the motor.

He slid out the far door on the side away from the road. Up ahead he could see the lights of cars being parked in an open field. When his eyes had become adjusted to the gloom (there was no moon) he saw several men standing beside their parked cars slipping on their robes. This cheered him so much he felt like shouting. He didn't need a membership card after all. He hurriedly opened his bundle and put on the robe and adjusted the helmet. He was astonished to learn how much difference these two simple pieces of cloth made on his emotions. The minute he had them on, his heart stopped jerking and his breathing became easier. He felt absolutely safe in this anonymity. He even smiled to himself under the helmet. It was amazing. He felt that he had made a great discovery: that this was why men conceal themselves in robes and ride the night. They feel absolutely safe.

He walked up the side of the road, towards the front . . .

In an open spot in a field, in a wide clearing, there was a great group of black-robed figures, several hundred of them, barely distinguishable in the darkness of the night. This was the old flying-field, the war-time flying-field, which had long since been abandoned. There was a single large hangar remaining, and through the cracks and apertures Dolan could see lights shining . . . he walked slowly over to the hangar.

The doors were open and he saw that there were several hundred robed figures inside standing around. At the side of one wall was a raised platform, crudely built, with a dozen or more chairs, the kind funeral parlours use.

He walked past the doors to the other side. Here there were a number of cars, thirty-five or forty, parked beside the hangar in precise rows – expensive cars: sedans, phaetons, coupés. These plainly belonged to important people. He strolled down past them . . . and at the end of the hangar, where the road came into the old flying-field, there were two men, in their robes, acting as traffic marshals, protecting this restricted parking area from the rank-and-file members. Dolan reflected for a moment on the irony of this discrimination in an organization whose number one article was Equality. Under his robe he took out a folded wad of paper and a pencil and began copying down the licence plates of the expensive cars. He could not see what he was doing, but he had plenty of room in which to write, and he was very careful to copy the numbers accurately.

. . . A whistle blew somewhere behind him, and at once there was a general movement towards the front of the hangar. He looked at his strap-watch. A few minutes to twelve. He walked along with the others, feeling elated about the licence plates. It would be a very simple matter now to find out who some of the Crusaders were.

The inside of the hangar was crowded, and the robed figures continued to pour through the big doors. Dolan pushed along towards the centre to a position almost directly in front of the

raised platform. Seven men were on the platform now, looking
down, and another one was going up the steps. Eight men.
They wore robes and helmets, identical with the hundreds of
men below them except for various insignia on the forehead of
their helmets, little symbols in white, marks of rank. They
resembled Greek letters, but they were so small, and Dolan
was so far away, that he could not make them out.

The officers on the platform whispered among themselves
for a few minutes, and then there was another shrill whistle
from the edge of the assembly. One of the officers signalled
with his hand and the big doors scraped and squeaked shut.
Instantly the hum of conversation among the hundreds of men
died down. The officer who had signalled with his hand took a
step forward on the platform, facing the men below, and ex-
tended his hand in a Hitler-gesture. Now there was dead silence.
The officer raised his hand, like a baton, whipped it downward,
nodding his head sharply:

> *'My country, 'tis of thee'*

they sang,

> *'Sweet land of liberty*
> *Of thee I sing.*
> *I love thy rocks and rills,*
> *Thy woods and templed hills,*
> *From every mountain-side,*
> *Let freedom ring!'*

The song swelled in a great burst of emotion and then died.
Every eye was on the men on the platform. Another officer
stepped forward, made a Hitler-gesture and then jerked his head
forward, bowing it. Dolan was aware that all around him the
members were bowing their heads, and he lowered his too, but
not so much that he couldn't see out of the tops of his eyes

what went on on the platform . . . the officials had their heads bowed, too.

'Oh! Gawd, our Heavenly Father,'

the preacher, the chaplain, said,

'We ask your blessing on this assembly tonight; let Thy wisdom continue to impress itself on these Crusaders, these noble name-sakes of mejeeval pilgrims who went forth across the Red Sea to do battle with the black infidels who dessecreated Thy temples; help us to be strong and brave and strike terror to the hearts of Thine enemies. Amen.'

The preacher, the chaplain, jerked his head up and stepped back. The assembly sighed audibly. Dolan smiled under his helmet, wondering how many of them knew the preacher, the chaplain, had muffed a couple of facts and a couple of words; and then the first officer, the interlocutor, stepped forward, standing still, waiting for the men to stop shifting. He finally held up his hand.

'A–a–at Ease!' he hollered.

The command boomed and rolled around the sheet-metal hangar.

'Crusaders,' he said, 'tonight marks the seventh meeting of this great organization. Day by day we are meeting the situations that we set out to correct, day by day we are achieving results. Day by day our ranks are being swelled by red-blooded Americans who come to us because they are sick and tired of the present method of law-enforcement, and because there are certain phases of every-day life over which the law and the courts have no control. America for Americans!'

'America for Americans!' roared the mob.

The officer made another quick Hitler-salute.

One of the other officers on the platform handed him a paper and he held it in front of him.

'Crusaders,' he said, 'Bulletin Number Seven. It is hereby ordered that an immediate boycott of the Zellerwein Brewery be put into effect. Reason: When members of the committee for the support of Otto Henry for Senator approached Mr Zellerwein and asked for contributions and his help in lining up his one thousand employees, Mr Zellerwein refused, threatened bodily harm to members of the committee. Although a naturalized American, Mr Zellerwein was born in a foreign country, and his ideas on good government naturally are subversive. The following stores and business houses also are ordered boycotted for good and sufficient reasons: The Midway Market, 1215 Endicott Boulevard; Mossman's Restaurant, 415 Sixth Street; Grayson's Dry Goods Store, on Southern Avenue – '

He paused as another officer came over to him and whispered something.

'I am informed,' he said, turning to the assembly, 'that three members of the Crusaders are employed at Grayson's. I want these three men to send the committee a full report on what the nature of their jobs is, how much money they earn, the size of their families, and how much money they have in the savings bank for emergencies. The committee will try to place these men in a store that is favourable for our cause. The boycott list will be available after the meeting is over, and I want every man here to memorize the names and addresses of the stores and positively do no business with them in any respect under threat of punishment. The three men who work at Grayson's may continue there until further notified by the committee.

'And now – Abraham Washington!' he barked, turning his head.

There was a movement below the platform, the dull sounds of scuffling feet, and then the wails of a man. In a moment two Crusaders went up the steps half-dragging a Negro man of about fifty years. They took him to the platform and turned him loose, stepping back. The Negro took a look at those hundreds of robed figures below him and started moaning. You could not understand what he was saying.

The officer looked at him.

'Abraham Washington!' he said. 'You have been heard to condemn the present system of county relief many times. You are a disorganizer – '

'Boss man, boss man,' the Negro said, 'I didn't mean it. Boss man, I swear to God I didn't mean it. I all is – '

'You have been disturbing the Negro people of your neighbourhood, inciting them to protest. The Crusaders See All Know All. You bear the names of two great immortal Americans – and we are going to teach you how to respect them – '

'Boss man, boss man – '

'Negroes must be taught to stay in their places. This lesson we are going to teach you will not be fatal – but if you do not keep your mouth shut you will be hanged next time from the rafters of this building.'

'Tar and feathers!' the officer roared.

'Ay–ay–ay–ay!' the Crusaders yelled, applauding.

Two more Crusaders started up the steps, followed by a third one. They carried an ordinary wash-tub between them, with heavy cloths run through the handles so they would not burn their hands. The bottom of the tub was blackened by some. The man behind carried a large sack and a big kalsomining brush. They proceeded to the middle of the platform and stopped.

'Undress him,' the officer ordered.

Abraham Washington, the Negro, offered no resistance. He was rolling his head, moaning.

'I could take a shot at those bastards right now,' Dolan said to himself, feeling his gun. 'I could pick off six of them – '

The Crusaders who had brought up the tar and feathers finally got the Negro's clothes off, all but his shoes and socks. Dolan could see the muscles trembling and jerking under the black skin.

The officer made another Hitler-salute. One Crusader stuck the brush in the tar and started swabbing the Negro, who was still rolling his head, moaning, but not actually crying out. When the swabbing was finished, two of the Crusaders reached into the sack and took out handfuls of feathers, throwing them on the Negro. There was a shower of feathers . . . and gradually the black body disappeared, and the symmetry of a human form disappeared and the Negro more and more resembled some grotesque bird. The chief officer himself delivered the *coup-de-grâce*. He shoved the brush into the tar, slapped it across the Negro's face, then took a double-handful of feathers and shoved them at his head.

'Take him away,' he said.

The Crusaders turned Abraham Washington around and started him down the steps . . . the others picked up the tub and brush and followed. The other Crusaders, standing below the platform, hollered and applauded . . . and in a moment everything was calm and peaceful again.

The officer stepped forward and saluted.

'America for Americans!'

'*America for Americans!*' they answered.

Dolan did not say anything. His lips were pressed tightly together.

'Arnold Smith!' the officer called.

Arnold Smith climbed the stairs, surrounded by three Crusaders, the guards. He was about forty, dressed in cheap clothes, a little good-looking. His face was sullen.

'Face the Crusaders,' the officer said.

Arnold Smith turned, facing the assembly. Dolan was studying his face. There was no sign of emotion, only that dark, sullen mask.

'Three times you have been warned by the committee on morals,' the officer said. 'You are notorious – '

'Men,' Arnold Smith said quietly, addressing the assembly, 'this fellow is wrong – '

'Shut up!' the officer barked.

'I don't know what's going to happen to me,' Arnold Smith said to him, still in a quiet tone, 'but I'm going to explain what happened. Men,' he continued, 'I admit I knocked up a girl. I paid for the operation. Just like a lot of you fellows have done. Only she happened to be the sister of – '

The guards grabbed him, slapping their hands over his mouth. Arnold Smith made no effort to free himself. The guards continued to hold him.

'This man,' the official said, 'is a menace to every young girl in the Bay Shore district. He has been warned three times to reform, let women alone. He has disregarded every warning. This, Crusaders, is the very situation we were organized to meet. The law can do nothing to this man, although he is guilty of loose morals. We must teach him a lesson – '

'Ay–ay–ay–ay!' they roared.

The officer gestured with his hand. Two other officers quickly stepped forward. One of them held a small black satchel. He opened it, took out a can and an ether mask. Two other officers moved out a small table. Arnold Smith was pulled towards the table. Suddenly he saw what was about to happen, and with a tremendous surge he threw off the guards and stood free, a look of horror on his face. He hesitated, looking about, then leaped from the platform into the crowd.

There was pandemonium in front of Dolan.

'All right, all right,' the officer on the platform said, holding out his hands, trying to quiet them. 'He'll be handled. Bring him up here,' he shouted.

Several men took Arnold Smith back up the steps, over-powering him. They bent him down on the table, still holding him, and the officer slapped the mask over his nose and started pouring out the ether . . . and in a couple of minutes Arnold Smith had ceased to struggle. The Crusaders stepped back, coming down the stairs to their places in the crowd.

'Now, you shall see what happens to men who menace the

morals of this community,' the officer said. 'Severe punishment, yes. But absolutely necessary to protect our homes – to protect your own sisters – '

He nodded to the officer with the satchel, and the entire staff of Crusaders on the platform crowded around the table, hiding it from the sight of the crowd. Behind the bodies, Dolan could see the officer moving his arms . . . and several times he caught the reflection of the overhead light on the scalpel. . .

Dolan said nothing to himself, thought nothing. His brain was a cold mass of cells. He knew it would be preposterous to try to stop this. It would be suicide. He started moving towards the doors, shifting his position a foot at a time, so as not to attract attention. But nobody noticed him. They were too interested in what was happening on the platform.

Bishop shook his head, biting his lip.

' "My country 'tis of thee," ' he said. 'My God, this is incredible. You can't write this story, Mike. Nobody'll believe it – '

'They'll believe it when I produce Arnold Smith – '

'How're you going to find him if he's not in the phone book? It's a cinch they wouldn't risk putting him in a hospital.'

'I'll find him. I'll comb that goddam Bay Shore district from top to bottom. I'll find him, all right – '

'My God!' Bishop said again, sighing, rubbing his hand over his face. 'I marvel that you didn't shoot 'em down – goddam sonofabitching sadists. That's what your capitalism does to men – makes swine of 'em. Well – maybe I won't live to see it, but I'll die happy knowing that the movement is on the way – '

'This'll give you a real bang,' Dolan said, handing him a list.

Bishop read a few names and addresses and looked up.

'What are these?'

'The leaders of The Crusaders – '

'How'd you get 'em?'

'Poetic justice. They had a special parking place by the

hangar, and I saw a lot of expensive cars there and I wrote down the licence plates. First thing this morning I went to police headquarters and looked 'em up in the book. And there they are – '

Bishop was astonished.

'You sonofabitch!' he said.

'Go on. Read the rest of them – '

Bishop finished reading the list, gasping.

'It's a Blue Book. It's a *Who's Who* – '

'That'll look good in print, won't it?'

'My God, yes. It'll do as much damage as an air raid – Boy, you had an inspiration when you copied those licences.'

'That was lucky. I didn't pay much attention to it at the time. It was not until this morning that it dawned on me. Look. You make a copy of that list and stash it away. I'm going out to try to find Arnold Smith – '

'How about me going with you?'

'No – '

'All right, I'm not going to argue with you. But I suppose you know that every day we get closer to the blow-off. Remember Carlisle – '

'I'm not worried about Carlisle. Not now.'

'All right. I wish you would keep in touch with us by phone. So we would have a rough idea of where you were – '

'I will. When Myra comes tell her to get that society dope together. We may go to press a couple of days early – '

'Sure. Say, what happened to your head? Where's the bandage?'

'Doctor cut it off this morning.'

'Looks funny to see you without the turban – '

'It feels funny. Like I was undressed. Better get Myra on that Little Theatre story too. You know the one I mean – '

'Want to bring in the Menefee angle?'

'Might as well. I want to write a follow on Tim Adamson, too. Poor bastard. Look out for things for a while – '

'What about your creditors? Forgotten that ad. you ran yesterday?'

'I'll be back for that. I wouldn't miss that for the world – '

He went downstairs and out into the street. As he was getting into his car Grissom yelled good morning to him. Dolan waved back and started the motor, turning around in the middle of the block, heading for the Bay Shore district.

The Bay Shore district was a middle-class neighbourhood. It depended for support on two big furniture factories. You could smell the factories when you crossed the viaduct and started down the hill to the reclaimed flatlands.

Dolan stopped at one factory and went into the time-keeper's office, introducing himself as a reporter from the *Times-Gazette* and asking for information on Arnold Smith. The time-keeper looked through the records and said he was sorry, no Arnold Smith worked there, or had worked there within two years. Dolan thanked him and went to the other factory.

The time-keeper here said a man named Arnold Smith had been employed about six months ago but was laid off now. Dolan asked him to describe him. The time-keeper chewed a pencil and gave a brief description.

'Sounds a little like him,' Dolan said. 'Can you give me his address?'

The time-keeper looked at the card.

'Three-one-five Perry Street. What do you want with him?' he asked, curious.

'He's come into a lot of money. Three-one-five Perry Street. Thanks.'

Dolan drove to 315 Perry Street. It was a small one-storey bungalow. A woman of about sixty answered the knock at the door.

'Pardon me,' Dolan said. 'Is this where Arnold Smith lives?'

'Yes,' the old woman said. 'I'm his mother. What did you want to see him about?'

'I'm not sure he's the Arnold Smith I'm looking for,' Dolan

said. 'Do you mind if I come in a minute?'

'No, come in,' Mrs Smith said, opening the door.

Dolan went inside to the small hall.

'My name's Dolan,' he said. 'Could I see Mr Smith?'

'He's not here. What did you want to see him about?' Mrs Smith said, beginning to look worried.

'I only wanted to speak to him a minute. Ask him a few questions – '

'Are you the man who telephoned him last night? Are you the man who was going to give him the job?'

'That's what I wanted to see him about,' Dolan said, trying to make his voice casual.

'What business have you got with him? Where is he?' Mrs Smith asked nervously.

'Have you got a picture of him that I could look at – '

'Mister, what's the matter . . .'

'Now, don't be alarmed, Mrs Smith,' Dolan said, showing his deputy's badge. 'I'm from the sheriff's office. He's not in trouble or anything, but I'd like to see a picture of him. This may not be the Arnold Smith I'm looking for – '

The old woman stood and looked at him a moment, a deep frown on her forehead, and then she moved into another room. Dolan lit a cigarette and was surprised to discover that the palm of his hand was as wet as if he had touched it in a bowl of water . . . The old woman came back and handed him a picture.

Dolan looked at it closely.

'Is this Arnold Smith?' he asked.

'Yes. My son.'

'I'm awfully sorry to have caused you any trouble, Mrs Smith,' he said, handing back the picture. 'This isn't the man I'm looking for. Thank you . . .'

He went out, wondering if he'd done right in lying to the old woman.

He drove back across the viaduct, stopped at a drug-store and

had a coke and telephoned the office. Bishop said there was
nothing new except that Ox Nelson had been by and had left
word that he wanted to see him. And, oh yes, a special delivery
letter from Mrs Marsden, thanking him for the repayment of
the loan. The letter was from Los Angeles. Myra was there,
getting the stuff together, and did he find Arnold Smith?

Dolan said no, he'd located his mother, but that it was a long
story and he'd tell him when he came in. He hung up and called
police headquarters and asked for Lieutenant Nelson. The
lieutenant seemed delighted to hear from him. He had something important to talk to him about and could he come right
over? No, no, it couldn't possibly wait. There was a peremptory
quality in the lieutenant's tone. Dolan said all right, he'd come
by.

'Now look here, Mike, for God's sake, be reasonable. You're
out of diapers,' Nelson said, getting up from his desk, looking
at Dolan.

'How'd you find out all this?' Dolan asked.

'Find it out! I'm head of the Red Squad, ain't I? How the
hell do you suppose I found it out?'

'Boloney!' Dolan said. 'Who told you?'

'Don't start asking me questions. Never mind who told me.
That dame and Ed Bishop are a couple of goddam Communists,
and you'd better tell 'em what's what or I'll pull 'em in on a
morals charge.'

'You tell me to be reasonable, I tell you to be reasonable. Ed
Bishop's the same guy he's been for fifteen years. He was that
way when he was on police, and you know it. Why have you
suddenly decided to get him out of town?'

'You answer me a question,' Nelson said. 'What do you know
about this Barnovsky dame? Nothing. She blew in out of nowhere and goes to work for you. You're a chump. She's done
time in Texas for distributing radical literature. She's working
right out of Moscow. She didn't tell you that, did she?'

'I asked you why you'd suddenly decided to get Ed Bishop out of town,' Dolan said again.

'I don't have to answer your silly questions,' Nelson said. 'I'm telling you what to do. Look, Mike. I like you. All the boys up here like you. And these two people are friends of yours. That's why I'm letting you break the news instead of going down there myself – '

'You were down there an hour ago. Why didn't you tell 'em then?'

'Hell,' Nelson said angrily, 'that's what I been trying to explain to you. They're friends of yours, goddam it.'

'All right, Ox – I'll tell 'em. I don't think it'll do any good, but I'll tell 'em. And now, do me a favour. Who started all this?'

'I can't tell you that, Mike. All I can tell you is that it comes from pretty high up.'

'An order?'

'Hell, you can laugh them off. This was more than an order – '

'Carlisle?'

'I'm not saying – '

'I didn't know he has a hand in the police department. I thought Emmett hated his guts – '

'I'm not saying – '

'All right,' Dolan said, smiling, getting up. When he was finally erect the smile faded from his face. 'You know, Ox,' he said, 'you're the biggest sonofabitch I ever met in my life – '

Nelson blinked his eyes, and his mouth went in and out in half-smiles that kept turning into sneers.

'On the level,' Dolan said coldly. 'You're a sonofabitch – '

He turned and walked out.

When he got back to the office he found Bud McGonagill waiting for him.

'Hello Bud,' Dolan said.

'I want to talk to you,' McGonagill said.

'Here, or you want to go downstairs?'

'Here'll do,' McGonagill said shortly. 'What the hell did you do to that old woman on Perry Street?'

'Do to her? What do you mean, do to her?'

'Nix, nix – she telephoned the office and said a deputy named Dolan was out to see her. Thank God I answered the phone myself. She cried and moaned over about something happening to her son. She said somebody called there last night and talked to him about a job, and then he left. What the hell is this all about?'

'You know as much as I do. I did go out there to see a Mrs Smith, looking for her son. I flashed my badge on her because that was the only way I could get to see a picture of him – '

'Get it?' Bishop said sarcastically to McGonagill.

Dolan motioned for him and Myra to keep quiet.

'What did you want to see the picture for?'

'To identify him. I wanted to see if I knew him.'

'Did you?'

'Sure, but I told the old lady I didn't. I was afraid I'd upset her.'

'Well, she's plenty upset now. What about the guy? Who is he? He's been reported missing. I've got to find him – '

'I'd like to find him myself, but I'm afraid he'll be missing until he gets well. He had an operation performed last night – '

'Where is he now?'

'I wish to God I knew,' Dolan said.

'What kind of an operation?'

'What do you think?'

'What?' McGonagill exclaimed.

'The Crusaders. Those noble Crusaders – '

' "My country 'tis of thee," ' Bishop sang softly.

'Hell!' McGonagill said. 'That's what the old lady meant. She said right after you left, somebody telephoned and said he was the man who had spoken about the job the night before.

He said Arnold was going away to South America and wouldn't have time to telephone, he was busy getting his new stuff, but that he would write from New Orleans. That's evidently what upset the old lady so much. She couldn't figure out why her son wouldn't at least telephone her good-bye.'

'She couldn't figure it out,' Dolan said; 'but we can. You know what that means, don't you? Arnold Smith's dead – '

'The odds are he's not, but this is a mess,' McGonagill said. 'Men don't die from that – '

'Not all of 'em do,' Dolan said slowly. 'Not all of 'em. But Arnold Smith did, as sure as God made little green apples. Yes, sir – as sure as God made little green apples, he's dead – '

'Well . . .' McGonagill said.

'Bud, there's nothing you can do but sit tight and hope for the best,' Dolan said. 'You've got nothing to worry about until somebody stumbles across the body – if they ever do. You've been square as hell with me and I appreciate it, and I'll try to keep this thing from reaching you. I don't know where it's going to lead myself – but I'm in this thing up to my eyes, and I'm going through with it – '

McGonagill turned and went down the steps without a word. Dolan watched him go through the door to the street. Then he leaned over the railing, looking down.

'Grissom,' he said, 'get those goddam pressmen in here early tomorrow morning.'

That afternoon at three o'clock his creditors came in ones, twos, and threes to collect their bills. They congratulated him and said they thought his advertisement in the paper was very clever. It was rather a flat occasion for Dolan. He had waited a good many years for this moment, but he got no more kick out of the actual ceremony than he did the ad. he had run the day before. Finally, they were all gone.

'You're a bad guesser,' Myra said. 'There's a little more than five thousand dollars left – '

'I knew there would be,' he said, picking up the money, putting it in his pocket. 'Come on – '

'What are you talking about? We've got work to do if we're going to press in the morning – '

'We'll be back in thirty minutes. Come on – '

'Where? Where are we going?'

'Come on. We're going to get married. I'm going to marry you – '

'Mike,' Bishop said, 'have you gone crazy?'

'Come on . . .' Dolan said to Myra.

Dolan laid down the proofs he was reading and got up off the bed, going to the door. It was Ulysses.

'Beg your pardon, Mister Mike,' he said, 'but we're moving tomorrow, and – '

'I can always tell when you want money, Ulysses. How much?'

'Well, sir – the moving man said it'd be twenty dollars to take two loads, but I think we got about four – '

Dolan took out a fifty-dollar bill and handed it to him.

'That's for moving – not for some high yaller.'

'Yes, sir. We got a nice new place, Mister Mike. You ain't seen it yet, have you?'

'No. Ernst told me about it tonight.'

'You got the best room, Mister Mike. I saw to that myself. I got to sort of take care of you since you're so busy – '

'Yeah. Thanks, Ulysses. Now beat it – '

'Yes, sir,' Ulysses said, going out. 'I'll have your room all fixed tomorrow night. It's funny, Mister Mike,' he said, pausing at the door, 'but there won't be much of this old house left this time tomorrow night. They started tearing down the back end this afternoon.'

Dolan went back to the proofs and in a few minutes Bishop and Myra came in.

'The second Mrs Michael Dolan,' Bishop said, holding out

Myra's hand, 'brought back to the master's bed safe and sound, her belly full of ham sandwiches and malted milks – a goddam plutocrat.'

'This stuff reads all right to me,' Dolan said, indicating the proofs. 'What did you think of it?'

'Swell story,' Bishop said. 'But, hell, that yarn doesn't have to be beautifully written. It's so big it'll carry itself. Hear anything more from Mrs Smith?'

'I phoned her a little while ago. She's heard nothing. Hell, that fellow's dead. After we bust this story they'll find his body – '

'Unless it's been cremated,' Myra said.

'I thought of that. Then I promptly forgot it. They wouldn't do that. That's murder.'

'It's murder anyway,' Myra said.

'Well, I'm glad we've finally nailed Jack Carlisle. And Thomas, too. I never would have suspected him – '

'What about Crenshaw? Past president, Chamber of Commerce – '

'Carlisle's the one I'm tickled about. Especially since Nelson – '

'Nelson. What about Nelson?'

'I'm coming to that,' Dolan said. 'That's why I wanted you to come here tonight. Nelson read the riot act to me this morning – '

'About me?' Bishop asked.

'About the both of you – '

'So that's what he wanted to talk to you about!'

'That was it. He said you had to get out of town or else – '

'He's bluffing – '

'No, he's not. He's got orders from somebody. A command. From Jack Carlisle. This is the beginning of Carlisle's revenge – '

'Why didn't you tell us this before?' Myra asked.

'Oh, I didn't want to annoy you. I put it off as long as I could – '

'I see now why you married me,' Myra said.

'Sit down and shut up a minute,' Bishop said.

'That's why you married me, isn't it? Isn't it?'

'Well – '

'That is the reason, isn't it?'

'You're taking this the wrong way,' Dolan said, trying to find words to explain.

'You bastard,' Myra said, slapping him hard in the face.

Dolan's lips went together, but he said nothing, standing there looking at her. She slapped him again in the face, a little harder. Bishop lunged at her, grabbing her around the waist, the force of the lunge carrying them both sprawling across the bed.

'I'll break your jaw,' Bishop growled.

Dolan had not moved.

'Ed,' he said quietly.

Bishop got to his feet. Myra suddenly rolled over on her stomach and began to cry.

'Ed,' Dolan said, taking a big roll of money out of his pocket, 'here's five thousand. You'd better take the family and move – '

Bishop smiled, then grinned, then laughed.

'No,' he said, shaking his head.

'Take it,' Dolan said, holding out the money.

'No – '

Dolan suddenly shoved the roll of bills into Bishop's coat pocket.

'Use your head,' Dolan said.

'I'm sticking, Mike,' Bishop said, taking the money out of his pocket. 'Take back this dough or I'll throw it out the window. So help me God, I will.'

Myra had stopped crying, was sitting up on the bed.

'Wait a minute, Ed. That's for the kids. I know they need a lot of things. That money's for them – medicine, doctors – '

Bishop let the hand holding the money fall to his side.

'I'm sticking,' he said doggedly.

'You take that money home to your wife. Tell her it's for her – '

'Okay – but I'm sticking.'

'You're a goddam fool,' Dolan said.

The telephone rang.

'Should I?' Bishop asked.

Dolan nodded and Bishop went out.

'Get up from there and cut out that monkey-business,' Dolan said to Myra. 'For God's sake, I didn't mean to make you sore. I was only trying to help you – '

'I've been sitting here wondering about you,' Myra said. 'Do you mind if I see your hands?'

Dolan went over and held out his hands. She turned them over looking at the palms. Then she looked up at him smiling, with fresh tears in her eyes.

'What?' he asked, puzzled.

'I was looking for the scars of the nails,' she said.

Bishop came back, excited.

'I damn near booted it. I told her you weren't here. She's on the phone,' he said.

'Who?'

'Mrs Smith. She wants to talk with you – '

Dolan went out.

'Why don't you try to be nice to the guy?' Bishop said to Myra. 'Don't be stupid all your life. This Mick is the swellest sonofabitch that ever came down the pike. He's in love with you – '

'He's got a peculiar way of showing it,' Myra said.

'Well, he is, anyway. Why don't you try to get along with him?'

'I will – '

'I ought to knock both your heads together – '

Dolan rushed back in the room.

'Arnold Smith's home,' he said, his eyes bright. 'He's just

turned up. This cinches the case. I know he'll help us. I'm going out and have a talk with him – '

'We'll all go,' Bishop said. 'All of us – '

'Want to?' Dolan asked Myra.

'Sure,' she said, getting up.

'That's more like it,' Bishop said. 'Come on – '

The *Cosmopolite* broke the story late that afternoon, with names and facts. Dolan had purposely held back the distribution until after four o'clock when he was certain the editorial and mechanical staffs of the afternoon newspapers had quit for the day. He was taking no chance of a remake on any one of their final editions.

LEADING CITIZENS OF TOWN HEAD CRUSADERS

JACK CARLISLE AND CRENSHAW LEAD MASKED MOB WHICH

MUTILATES BAY SHORE MAN

ASTOUNDING EXPOSURE OF SECRET SOCIETY

IN THE COSMOPOLITE — OUT NOW —

read placards all over town.

Dolan tried to buy five-minute periods on the three radio stations, had offered to pay for a regular fifteen-minute period, but it was no go when he told them what he wanted to talk about. He was in a frenzy of hatred. He wanted everybody in town to know about it. By six o'clock everybody did. People buzzed in the streets, the telephone wires hummed, the press association teletypes were clicking . . . Even had an anonymous mob mutilated Arnold Smith it would have been a good story. But when the leaders of the mob were known, when their names were set double-column in a full-page box, it became one hell of a story. In one thrust, Dolan had knocked the town upside down.

. . . Dolan was alone in the office when he heard a rattle at the back door. He went down and let in Bud McGonagill.

'For God's sake, get out of here,' he said. 'I just come from the courthouse, and Judge Pentland has called a special session of the Grand Jury. They're on their way down now – '

'That's what I wanted,' Dolan said. 'I'll talk to 'em – '

'Put it off until in the morning,' McGonagill said. 'Hide out somewhere. Take time to get your facts straight – '

'My facts are straight. They're all in the magazine. And I've got Smith staked out, too – where I can get him when I want him. We're ready – '

'Mike, for God's sake, I'm trying to tip you off. I ducked because they're making out a subpoena for you right now – don't go around that courthouse tonight. There's no telling what'll happen – '

'Listen, Bud – '

'You mule-headed sonofabitch, you can't appear tonight. Wait until in the morning. Then telephone me and I'll come out with some men and give you protection. You don't seem to understand – you've blasted this town wide open. Hell, you've got people involved you never dreamed of – judges and even a Congressman – you've got to get away from here – '

'All right,' Dolan said finally. 'I'll leave here, but I'm going home. By God, if anybody tries to start anything with me I'll start something with them. I haven't forgotten how to shoot – '

'I don't care where the hell you go – but get out of here. This is the first place they'll come to – '

'All right, Bud. Thanks. You better go now.'

'You swear you're leaving here?'

'Just as soon as I get my coat – '

'And you'll call me first thing in the morning?'

'I swear that, too – '

'Goddam you, why are you grinning? Do you think I'm kidding? Don't you realize Carlisle doesn't care about what the magazine says if he can keep you from talking? He can laugh off that magazine story – '

'The hell he can – '

' – I can't afford to stay any longer, Mike.'

'All right, Bud, go ahead. I don't think you're kidding. I'm going as soon as I get my coat. I was supposed to meet Grissom and Bishop and Myra here at seven o'clock, but I'll leave – '

'So long – '

'So long.'

Dolan watched him go out the back door and then he went upstairs and got his coat. He went into the office and switched on the light and telephoned the new house. Ulysses answered and said Miss Myra was right there.

'Hello, babe,' Dolan said. 'Look. McGonagill was just here, pretty excited by the situation at the courthouse. The Grand Jury is going to have a special session to investigate The Crusaders and he didn't want me to appear tonight. . . He wants me to wait until tomorrow morning when I can have a body-guard. How's that – getting up in the world, hunh? . . . God, you're worse than he is. . . What the hell, I'm not scared. I've been waiting for this. So get hold of Bishop and Grissom and tell them not to come back, but meet me at the house. How do you like the new house? . . . That's good. . . Sure, I'm leaving now. Bye, babe – '

He hung up, turned off the lights in the office and went to the front door. He turned off the overhead light and started out the front door when he changed his mind, closed the front door and went back to the rear door.

He opened it and went out, slamming it behind him. He started down the alley to the parking station. At the corner, in the darkness, he stumbled over a small box a little out from the trash pile in the rear of the cheap café. When he regained his balance he was against a garbage can that had no lid, and he smelled the sour odour of orange rinds and coffee grounds.

'Sonofabitch!' he exclaimed, not because he had stumbled, but because he had smelled the uncovered garbage. *Coffee grounds* . . . 'This is funny,' he said to himself, and then he heard a rustle behind him, and for no reason that he could understand he was suddenly frightened as he had never been frightened before; wild, animal fright. Before he could move he felt a touch on the brim of his hat in back, and then he knew that something horrible was about to happen, that he was but a rapid heart-beat away from death. The end of the alley and the tiny point of light that meant safety were a million miles away. A cry of terror sprung into his throat, but before he could utter it his ear-drums exploded and the point of light that was the alley rushed towards him with terrifying speed, red and roaring and utterly unstoppable. He knew he was being murdered, and he could think but one thought: Suppose Myra *had* stopped that day for that cup of coffee?

Then the top of his head flew off, and he fell face downwards across the garbage can, trying to get his fingers up to hold his nose.

Also by Horace McCoy and published by Serpent's Tail

THEY SHOOT HORSES, DON'T THEY?

The depression of the 1930s led people to desperate
measures to survive. The Marathon Dance Craze, which
flourished at that time, seemed a simple way for people to
earn extra money—dancing the hours away for cash. But,
the underside of that Craze was filled with a competition
and violence unknown to most ballrooms. Horace McCoy's
classic American story captures that dark side in this
powerful novel.

"Language is not minced in this short novel which
presents life in its most brutal aspect. So if you don't
like that kind of book, don't read it."
—*Saturday Review of Literature*

" . . . sordid, pathetic, senselessly exciting . . . It has
the immediacy—and the significance—of a
nerve-shattering explosion."
—*The New Republic*

"Were it not in its physical details so carefully
documented, it would be lurid beyond itself."
—*The Nation*

KISS TOMORROW GOODBYE

Kiss Tomorrow Goodbye is a kind of success story. A Phi Beta Kappa scholar succeeds in turning himself into a vicious and completely immoral criminal—a man whose contempt for law, order, and human life drives him relentlessly into a career of unrelieved evil. He escapes from a chain gang to join a pack of gangsters and a millionaire's daughter falls in love with him, but eventually his past overtakes him. *Kiss Tomorrow Goodbye* is McCoy's most ambitious work and the basis for one of the great gangster movies, starring James Cagney.

"One of the nastiest novels ever published in this country."
—*Time*

"This will probably be quarantined from libraries, but in action-adventure of the late '20s, this has a literate, nerve-lacerating, whip-lashing effectiveness. Doublecheck it."
—*Kirkus Reviews*

I SHOULD HAVE STAYED HOME

The acclaimed exposé of Hollywood in the 1930s: the
gigolos, the starlets, the fan magazines and the despair
behind the glitter. *I Should Have Stayed Home* tells the story
of two jobless roommates and movie extras, Ralph Carson
and Mona Matthews. After Mona gains notoriety for cursing
a judge during a friend's trial, she and Ralph are introduced
to Hollywood society. Ralph battles with his own corruption
and loss of principle, while Mona serves as his conscience,
warning him against himself and the temptations of success.

"The background, the talk and the vague ending are
all realistic, and tough-minded readers seeking the
truth about Hollywood's lower depths will not object
to the violent language used to express it."
—*The New York Times Book Review*

"...A true picture... McCoy is talking to the kids who
come in flocks to become stars, the kids who never
read books like this."
—*Times Literary Supplement*